When Love Unlocks Time

Copyright © Camilla Cornish 2017

ISBN: 9781521291467

All rights reserved. This book or any portion thereof may not be reproduced or used in any manner whatsoever without the express written permission of the publisher except for the use of brief quotations in a book review.

First Printing: 2017 Spearmint Books Isle of Man

spearmint@manx.net

+44 1624 838001

◆◆◆

Chapter One
The Key

Carefully edging around the periphery of the scene being shot, Miranda found her way to a quiet dim corner of the great hall. She meticulously arranged the yards of fabric of the skirt of her authentic Tudor gown as she sank down onto the stone bench that was built in to the alcove. She could still hear the film crew if she was called but was totally hidden from view and she felt the relief of solitude flooding through her.

It took her eyes a few moments to adjust to the lack of light and even then she could only see the vaguest outline of what looked like a dark line running down the wall. Curiously, she ran her fingers along the line and then suddenly stood up to trace its path more thoroughly. There was definitely something there, a blocked-up window came to mind, but this wasn't an external wall.

'it's a door'

Miranda whispered the words, she wasn't sure who she was hiding it from but every instinct told her not to draw attention to what she had found. Carefully and silently feeling her way, she found the place where the handle should be. There was no handle but there was a tiny key in a lock, incongruously fragile when compared with the solidity of the alcove and walls.

Slowly she turned the key, she knew that the strict rules they had been given regarding their historic surroundings would have made this off limits but who could have resisted?

It felt like an eternity before the ground beneath her started to right itself as her mind struggled to make sense of what was happening, she had been flung to the floor by the intensity of the sound that had roared through her mind and body, it was as if a savage gale had lifted her from the calm and thrown her into a whirlwind. The colour started to return to her cheeks as violently as it had left and she heard the music playing, oh no, she had missed the cue! Turnover in the world of film extras was indifferently ruthless and a blunt, 'not required again' would mean she couldn't make her share of the rent this month.

Still feeling shaken, Miranda put on her beautiful jeweled mask and headed back into the hall, there were a lot of people in this scene and there was a chance she could slip back in amongst the dancers unnoticed. The bowing, curtseying, smiling and dancing had begun in earnest. The fabulous gowns and richly coloured doublets and sleeves made a beautiful picture and the minstrels played as gaily as for a wedding. A man in a golden mask studded with rubies bowed to Miranda and said, 'may I have the honour of this dance my Lady?' Miranda knew straight away that this wasn't the same person she had been paired up with at rehearsals, maybe her allocated partner had been told to dance with someone else as she was late.   She curtseyed low and gave him her hand and he whisked her in amongst the dancers with energy and confidence, there was no doubt who was leading and she gave herself up to the dancing.

Miranda was wearing a beautiful forest green Tudor gown, sewn with wonderfully realistic pearls and diamonds, it was no hardship to be part of this wonderful world. Even the gorgeous square toed embroidered dancing slippers were completely authentic, making no allowances for the fact that left and right feet were differently shaped.

'May I know your name my Lady?'

She could tell that he was gorgeous, no mask could hide it. He was tall and muscular and he held her firmly but lightly, staying in character beautifully and Miranda responded in kind.

'My Lord! Tis a masked ball! Would you have me declare myself before the unmasking? You can only guess whether you are dancing with a kitchen maid or a mysterious Princess from foreign lands.'

He laughed and said, 'The sweetest perfume comes from your hair; indeed, I am unfamiliar with the scent, I am intrigued, will you tell me what it is?' His eyes were still twinkling, amused and flirtatious but as he asked the beautiful blue seemed to change colour, deepening as he genuinely seemed to want to know the answer.

'Why Lord, it is the finest coconut, brought over many lands and seas to perfume my hair'

'Coconut? I am unfamiliar with that word, what sort of nut is that and from whence does it come?' He seemed genuinely puzzled and interested. 'It is a large and fibrous nut Lord; it comes from a land many months' travel across dangerous seas.'

He was amazed now, 'Do you speak for my amusement Madam or is there truth in your words?'.

At that moment, the music finished, at once the room began to unmask and Miranda's shakiness rushed back as he revealed his unmistakable features, a face that had enthralled more ambitious women than Miranda. 'but, but, you're Henry VIII!' The King roared with laughter, delighted with his own success and her genuine shock.

He reached over and with the gentlest of touches he removed her mask, 'I bow before your beauty My Lady, no kitchen maid I think, please tell me your name.' Feelings of shock flooded her body and amongst the confusion she was still aware that his gaze made her feel like no-one else on earth existed, what was going on?

'Miranda, Your Majesty' she swept him a graceful curtsey as she spoke, her logical brain could not make sense of what was happening, maybe she was dreaming? Where were the cameras and crew? 'Miranda, that is not a name I am familiar with, you have quite startled me with your new words. It derives from the Latin Mirandus?'

She nodded silently, 'Then I will agree, indeed I do find you admirable and wonderful, you are well named Mistress Miranda'. At that moment, a courtier made his bow to the King and while he was momentarily distracted Miranda made a less than elegant dash for the secret alcove.

She heard the King call out and faces turned towards her. She broke into a run, panting with fear and exertion she disappeared into the shadows and frantically turned the key.

◆◆◆

Chapter 2

Was it a dream?

The roaring and whirling was not as bad this time, it took Miranda only a few minutes to re-orientate herself, leaning against the cool stone while things calmed down. Her heart thundered and her breath came in gasps, what the hell had just happened? Miranda burst out of the alcove and ran back to where the people were sitting around the coffee station.

'What's up?' Tom wasn't the only one to notice that Miranda was upset, others looked around as her breath came in agitated gasps.

'Silence!' Janet, the assistant floor manager loved any chance to show that she was in charge and wasn't going to pass up on this one, Miranda had already annoyed her by looking like a princess from romantic tales of old in her dancing gown. Her sour face was puffed up with her estimation of her own importance. She looked towards the producer hoping for a nod of approval for her dedication to duty.

'Come on, it'll be OK', Tom led Miranda to a quiet spot behind the coffee station and whispered, 'What's happened? Are you ill?'

'I think, I think, I saw…, I must have been dreaming, I must have fallen asleep, I thought I danced with Henry VIII!'

Tom laughed quietly, 'You'll never get to dance with Henry VIII while the bulldozer is allocating the extras' parts, I think she'd like to give you the part of scullery maid with authentic rags! Are you feeling better now?'

'I think so, it was so real though Tom, I could smell the perfumes and wines and Henry asked me about my shampoo!' Tom couldn't help snorting with laughter, 'I think you need to start going to bed earlier, there's only so much sleeping you can do on the job'.

Miranda gradually settled down and was quite composed by the time she danced her dance, just as instructed, with the step perfect Lord she had been matched with at rehearsals.

At home later, Alice loved the story, 'Fascinating! That's got to mean something, to be aware of scents in a dream is pretty unusual! It's not really surprising that you dreamt about Henry VIII as you were meant to be at his ball. It's just the content is unexpected, talking to him about things that he wouldn't have known about.'

'What do you mean?' Miranda poured another glass of wine for them both.

'Well, you're the mediaeval history expert but I'm pretty sure that there were no coconuts in Britain in Tudor times and I definitely know that Shakespeare invented the name Miranda for The Tempest. At least you didn't want to marry him, you had the benefit of hindsight in advance there! Which wife was he on?'

'I don't know, there weren't any clues' Miranda tucked her legs underneath her, trying to recall the details.

'No clues! I thought you were the historian! Was he slim and irresistible or enormously fat and limping?'

Alice was as caught up in the Henry VIII dream as Miranda now, what a great friend she is thought Miranda, feeling a sudden rush of happiness that may or may not have had something to do with the second glass of wine.

'He was……. not slim but not fat, sort of muscular, gorgeous, and fascinating, definitely fascinating. I think that must place him around the Anne Boleyn time.'

'I have analysed your dream and will now give my considered judgment' Alice held out her hand for the kettle crisps.

'Go ahead, oh wise woman'

'I think it's time you got over Robert and came out with me on Saturday, being miserable was obviously phase one, dreaming about the most famously married man in history must be phase two, phase three comes into play when you meet someone who deserves you and you live happily ever after.'

Miranda laughed but not as easily as she had earlier, Robert had been a disaster it was true but it still hurt, not all the time but every now and then it would surge up again. The fact that she hadn't told him to get on his way the minute he started behaving like an entitled dickhead was what stung the most. Needing to tell people when to keep right on walking was not the same as being able to do it when it needed doing even though you knew it would make your life dramatically better. Better no relationship than lose her dignity again.

Later, Miranda thought back on the very long day. It had been no dream; it was either an incredibly vivid hallucination or…. No, the alternative just wasn't possible. Miranda gave up on trying to sleep and selected some of her research textbooks with images of Henry VIII at different points in his life. Bearing in mind that it was a very risky business to depict a king unfavourably, she thought that one of the Hans Holbein images was closest to when she had seen him, that would place him in the Anne Boleyn or Jane Seymour days.

Maybe it was the stress of waiting for the further study funding that was triggering all this. There was certainly no money coming from her late father's estate, even her allowance had ended when he died. Her stepmother had looked astounded when Miranda had mentioned it, as if the house the smug cow was sitting in hadn't been largely paid for by Miranda's mother's hard work.

What would her poor Mum have said if she could see her beloved daughter left with absolutely nothing? Miranda knew that she would have been furious and exasperated that her father had trusted his second wife to do the right thing by Miranda. His own trusting nature combined with the suddenness of his death at only fifty-eight had left financial matters in the hands of someone who didn't care about Miranda, a very vulnerable position to be in.

When Miranda overcame her embarrassment and raised the subject, her stepmother had expressed amazement that Miranda should expect to be supported at her age. Miranda wished that she didn't have such good manners, that she could be just as 'amazed' about her stepmother's source of income that kept her sitting very comfortably on her well upholstered backside.

Miranda pushed away the thought that maybe her own courage was lacking rather than her manners impeccable. What would Janet the bulldozer have done? Gone to war in every way no doubt. Legal or not.

There was no choice but to accept that there was no financial support, but Miranda was determined not to give up on her dream, to immerse herself even further into mediaeval history and its languages. She didn't care whether people like her stepmother thought it was a waste of time or not, it was Miranda's way of being in the world. Whatever had happened today there was no doubt that Miranda was going to check that door again tomorrow, at the very least she could see if it even existed.

◆◆◆

Chapter 3

The scullery maid

Miranda stood with the other extras who had been selected for scullery maids and was grateful for small mercies as she realised that the grease that was about to be rubbed into her hair was actually olive oil rather than the pure authenticity of well used kitchen grease. At least she didn't have to suffer the authentic aromas of the time. The blacking out of three teeth and streaks of smut across one cheek completed the look, it really wasn't a good one. If she wanted to think positive she could consider this a deep conditioning hair treatment, she would surely have the glossiest hair when she washed it off.

Janet the bulldozer had thoroughly enjoyed calling Miranda out of the dancers' group, Miranda would love to wipe the smirk off her face by flouncing out but she'd never get another day's work if she walked off a set.

Miranda used to wonder why some people were so unnecessarily awful but even she was forced to recognize jealousy when she encountered it so obviously. She felt that it was bizarre that the bulldozer had targeted her when you looked at the beauty of the women playing the main characters but bullies only bully when they think they can get away with it and Janet's sickening sycophancy around anyone she thought had a bit of power was pretty evident to those she thought she could lord it over which included all the Supporting Artistes. Miranda genuinely had no idea of her own quiet beauty and how it affected others.

The main actors were called to a scene first and Miranda could safely count on at least an hour before she would be needed. She quietly made her way to the hidden alcove and sat down for a moment to allow her eyes to adjust and to steady herself.

The violent rocking and swirling rushed in on her immediately, her hand leaning on the door helped a little and she was able to keep her thoughts clear enough to be glad that she had made sure she was sitting down. She quietly left the alcove and peeped around the edge of the wall.

People were dancing, the spectacle was just as beautiful as last time, as she watched enthralled she saw a tall man in a golden mask studded with rubies approach a modestly but beautifully dressed young girl in pastel blue with a silver and sapphire mask and make his bow to her. Miranda saw rather than heard the man say, 'May I have the honour of this dance My Lady?' she curtseyed low and kept her eyes sweetly downcast as he swept her into the dance and the musicians filled the room with extraordinarily rich music. As

Miranda started to realise that the music was familiar because she really had heard it before, a sharp slap across the side of her head was followed up by a furious hissing, 'what are you doing here you stupid girl? Get back to the kitchen!' The liveried servant dragged her to the nearest door and shoved her through it, she stumbled as he thrust an empty platter into her hands and said, 'take that back and stay there!' Miranda didn't dare go back to the dancing and make a run for the alcove, she followed the winding passageway and the racket of the kitchens reached her long before she reached the kitchens themselves. She unobtrusively put the platter down on the nearest table.

An immense crowd of people were working frantically in heat that almost knocked Miranda off her feet. As she tried to retreat into the passage, a red-faced woman shouted at her, 'why aren't you stoning them cherries? Get on with it!' she pointed angrily towards huge baskets piled high with glistening cherries.

'What all of them?' said Miranda, bewildered. The red-faced woman put her hands on her hips and looked astonished, 'Oh no your royal highness, why don't you pick out the dozen you like the look of and just do those? Only if it's not too much trouble of course.'

Those within earshot roared with laughter, Miranda flushed scarlet. A girl with a kindly face who was already seated on a stool at the cherry baskets took pity on Miranda even though she was laughing along with the rest of them.

'Sit with us' she said, 'we need to be quick about it though, I'll show you.' Miranda got to work and prayed that the red-faced woman wouldn't be doing any quality testing before she could get away.

'I'm Lizzie and this is Annie, what's your name?'

'Miranda' and she smiled nervously at the friendly face. 'Miranda! I've never heard of a name like that, you're not from these parts I 'll be bound.'

'That's right, I try to learn new ways quickly though'

'Safest way when Mrs Williams is in one of her tempers, she's not so bad though, we all get plenty to eat and scraps to take home if you're in favour.' Lizzie turned back to her friend and Miranda caught snatches of their conversation even though they had their heads close together.

Lizzie lowered her voice, 'They say that she never spends a night there now, so no bed linen to change and launder, always back by dawn though.' Annie spoke even lower, 'She is taking a great risk, I wouldn't like to bring the Queen's wrath down upon me' 'Things aren't the same since the real Queen's time.'

Lizzie looked around sharply, you never knew who was listening, best to be guarded, the kitchen was a hotbed of gossip though and Annie was keen to share her bit of news too. 'The upstairs servants reckon the one to look out for is the quiet one from the Seymour family, those who can see how the wind is blowing are making sure they keep well in with the Seymours'. Lizzie and Annie murmured together, dropping their voices even lower.

They were in a somewhat cooler part of the kitchen away from the central heat of the spits turning but Miranda could still feel the perspiration staining her dress and there was no mistaking the rancid smell of old cooking grease coming from Lizzie and Annie's hair and clothes. The cherry heaps had not much diminished but Miranda knew she must try and get back to the alcove, 'I must leave for a while Lizzie, I'm not too well' she left Lizzie feeling worried for her, Mrs William's temper would wear very thin if she saw a kitchen maid idling a second time.

Miranda made her way up the winding passage without meeting anyone, there was nothing for it at the door though, she couldn't get to the alcove without venturing out into the hall. Carefully she edged her way around the room, keeping her back against the wall and stepping into shadow whenever she could. She was almost there when she saw the incredulous face of the servant who had originally sent her to the kitchens, he couldn't believe his eyes at her bare faced cheek. He started towards her in a determined fashion.

Heart pounding, Miranda cut across the edge of the dancing space, cutting a strange figure in her rags as she darted past the silks and jeweled masks of the dancers. There was no doubt that it was the same dance as last time, she had returned at the exact same moment in time but this time the King had not danced with her, he had not noticed her existence in any way.

When she was feet from the alcove the servant grasped her roughly by the shoulder, 'Are you a simpleton? Get back to the kitchen and stay there!' her feet slipped from under her and she fell awkwardly, crying out as pain shot through her arm.

She saw a handsome man, richly dressed in deepest blue, raise his finger sharply to the man, 'Enough!' The liveried servant bowed low and Miranda made her move while he was distracted, she reached the door within seconds and as she touched the key the welcome roaring filled her head.

◆◆◆

Chapter 4
Making plans

Miranda helped herself to a coffee and sat down with the other kitchen extras, she was shaking but not as badly as last time, weird how the dancing extras and the kitchen extras didn't sit in the same group, maybe clothes really did maketh the man and woman, it was hard not to feel either glamorous or downtrodden when you were dressed that way.

She heard raised voices and could see various people gathering around the scene viewer, 'Why not? Where is she? Am I dealing with amateurs here? what about continuity!'

Everyone looked over to where Bulldozer Janet was obviously on the back foot, the producer's voice was raised again 'No, this is the one we are doing the close up on, it's decided, so make it happen!'

Minutes later Miranda found herself in the proper actors changing rooms having the fastest shower and hair dry of her life. The Bulldozer let her know that it was she who had decided to put her back in with the dancers but Miranda couldn't resist raising her eyebrows very slightly at this version of events, a small win maybe but very sweet.

The rush seemed to be just a continuation of the turmoil of the visit to Henry's Court as a kitchen maid, it was the strangest day!

This time Miranda concentrated on the rest of the filming and on her own dance scenes as if her life depended on it, she was going back again and this time she was going to be ready, any scrap of knowledge about the dances was going to be needed. She touched the tiny key that she had put on the fine chain around her neck and was hidden beneath her dress, she wasn't going to risk anyone else finding it, in either century.

Miranda spent the weekend refreshing her knowledge of King Henry's Court, it seemed likely that the time she was visiting was when King Henry was tiring fast of Anne Boleyn but had not yet formally begun Courting Jane Seymour. Miranda couldn't help smiling when she thought about how the King had only asked Jane to dance when she wasn't there.

She recounted her latest 'dream' to Alice who thoroughly enjoyed it, 'hold on! Who is this handsome chap at the end who saved you from the wicked maid beater? I like the sound of him.'

'I don't know' said Miranda thoughtfully, 'One of the dancers for sure so probably The Earl of somewhere or at least a Lord I should think, he was gorgeous, no doubt about that even if it wasn't my main concern at that moment'.

'Very interesting that you are having a classic damsel in distress dream, maybe you want saving from your extremely arid love life. Did you eat any of the cherries?'

'No I don't think so, why, what does it mean if you eat in a dream?'

'I don't know, I think it means you have to stay there but I may be thinking of Narnia!'

Miranda went over her research, it did cross her mind that maybe she was having some sort of breakdown that was resulting in a total disconnect with reality, but in her heart, she knew this was not the case. She had no intention of telling a single soul that she believed it was real, if she had lost her mind she'd kept enough of it to know that telling people she thought she was visiting Tudor England via a secret alcove was a one-way ticket to a secure institution.

So many thoughts competed in her mind, what did Henry like? How could she stay away for longer than an hour or so? Who on earth could she say she was? people didn't just turn up at Court with no-one to vouch for them.

Better be careful not to wash her hair in coconut shampoo. People who crossed Henry or Anne got their heads chopped off. Where could she tell Alice she was if she stayed away longer? Why did she want to dance with Henry again? And what about the thesis she could write? Never had anyone had an opportunity like this, every question that historians argued over she could find the definitive answer. And of course, there was the opportunity of the biggest plum of all time, she could bring back original documents and artifacts, or could she? She had the key but that had existed in this time. What would happen if she tried to bring something back with her? She'd come back with a bruised elbow right enough.

After several hours going over her research Miranda decided that what made Henry happy was power, adoration, maps, huge wealth, to be top dog over Charles of Spain and Francis of France, women, hunting, good food and especially music. She was also sharply reminded of the truth about Henry that had become obscured by his multiple marriages; he was a very clever, very learned, very seasoned King and statesman. With Charles of Spain and Francis of France hungry for power in Europe he had to be ready to defend his country, it was no mere clash of egos. Henry's ordering of the creation of the most accurate maps of the coastline ever created was a huge undertaking and an essential element in the defence of Britain, he needed to know where the weak spots were. His respect for Cromwell's work on this and the way he rewarded this humbly born man showed someone who knew worth when he saw it. In short, he was no-one's fool at this point in his life.

How utterly tragic that he had lost Katherine of Aragon and Cardinal Wolsey and would even eventually lose Cromwell, the rocks of wisdom and sage advice in his world. Yes, his own fault, but sometimes he seemed to Miranda to be like an enormous fish constantly swarmed by parasitic feeder creatures that would rather kill the host fish than give up on anything that benefitted themselves. Weirdly, Miranda felt a pang of tenderness for him, it bloody well was lonely at the top. 'What about your thesis that will catapult you into the top ranks of academics?' said one part of Miranda's mind, one dance and you've joined the 'what can Henry do for me?' camp too.

Henry liked gifts, Miranda had decided that she was going to go in for a penny in for a pound and when she went back through the door this time she would be armed with a back story and a gift for Henry. She thought about presenting herself as the survivor of a shipwreck and presenting Henry with a coconut but that would be a very risky strategy; sea-going and its spoils would most certainly arouse his interest but also his greed, potential thin ice indeed for someone who could get caught out at any time.

Miranda's next idea made her catch her breath, it was seriously audacious, but was it? How could she be caught out hundreds of years before something had happened? Almost as if someone was looking over her shoulder, she cautiously brought up Rudyard Kipling's poem IF on her screen and started to read. The outrageousness of her idea made Miranda close her eyes, to take one of the best loved poems in the world and present it to Henry VIII as her own creation!

That bit about walking with Kings might infuriate him and what about the blatant plagiarism? She had to remind herself several times that Rudyard Kipling wouldn't even be born at that point. Was there anyone who could be harmed by it? Looking at the first few lines of IF again, she realised that in Henry's time there was a very real danger of the 'losing heads' reference being taken literally.

Feeling as if she was about to be called in by the University Dean, she tried typing, 'IF you can keep your calm when all about you are losing theirs and blaming it on you' Miranda made her decision, she started searching online for specialist printers.

◆◆◆

Chapter 5

The first night – Summer 1535

As Friday's filming drew to an end and people started to get changed and return the costumes to the racks, Miranda, still in her dancing gown, took advantage of the hubbub and quickly put a day gown over her arm. She picked up the replica Tudor tapestry bag she had bought online from the British museum and stepped into the alcove. Out of sight, she added the gown to the other items in the bag and prepared herself for the sensation of going through the door.

On the other side of time, in the darkened alcove, she steadied herself and undid the beautiful glass bottle with the silver stopper she had bought from a vintage site. She dabbed her neck, shoulders and hair with the heady scents of jasmine and richer notes of honeysuckle, then she carefully left the bag deep in the shadows before she stepped out into the music.

Within minutes she was dancing with the man in the golden mask, loving the way he led with such confidence, making her feel as if she was a princess, caught up in a beautiful swirl of air, light and colour. Miranda had been careful to use gorgeously scented almond and lemon shampoo to wash her hair, it was a wise move, 'You wear the sweetest perfumes My Lady, I am intrigued, will you tell me what they are?' Her partner gracefully stepped through the dance as he spoke.

'Would you like to guess the fragrances My Lord?' Miranda loved the freedom the masked ball gave her to be bolder than she normally would, she knew that the King loved nothing more than for people not to recognize him and treat him as they would if he was not King.

'And if I am correct My Lady, what will you give me?'

'That must depend on whether I am a mysterious princess or a kitchen maid my Lord, it may be a poem that will be unlike any you have ever read before or it may be a cherry pie, which would you rather?'

'This is an unusual temptation Madam, I would be loath to choose between a poem and a pie made by your fair hand, maybe I could have both?'

'Indeed you drive a hard bargain my Lord!'

They swirled and dipped in the dance, Miranda was delighted that she was able to hold her own in both the dancing and the conversation, if the truth be told, with such a partner she could have followed him with even the smallest of natural talent.

'And what if you lose the challenge My Lord? What will my winnings be?'

'hmm, I am not used to losing, but it may be worth it to be the means of giving you pleasure. If I cannot tell you the perfumes then I will escort you in a walk in the Palace grounds tomorrow morning and pick the finest flower in the King's gardens to reflect your beauty, will that suit you?'

Miranda bowed her acceptance of the offer and the King said, 'I believe that the perfumes are daisies and buttercups' Miranda looked at him in a moment's amazement and then joined him in his delighted laughter as she conceded defeat and agreed that the morning's walk was his prize. At that moment, the music changed and she saw her partner signal to the minstrels and then remove his mask. 'But you are the King!' her amazement was still genuine, she was dancing with Henry VIII, it wouldn't ever seem real. After he had marveled at her name, he repeated his claim for the morning's walk.

On being told that she was staying in lodgings in the town, he immediately called a gentleman of the Court to his side and ordered him to arrange for her to stay at the Palace. He then excused himself with a splendid bow and returned to sit alongside the Queen who was resplendent in striking red with her pearl choker with the signature gold B at her throat. As Miranda watched him take his seat, she saw Anne Boleyn take note of it all and was sharply reminded that this was no game. People would be asking who she was, she hoped her back story would hold up.

Miranda was escorted to a seat by the handsome gentleman of the Court. Even without his striking deep blue doublet and sleeves, Miranda would have remembered him, the man who would care about someone striking a lowly kitchen maid was not soon to be forgotten. He introduced himself with a bow, his dark eyes and height were striking, his elegance barely concealing his powerful shoulders and arms, 'Lord Benedict Marchant at your service Mistress Glover. I will make arrangements and escort you to your apartment shortly, it is late and I am sure you are tired. Can I send to the town for your maid?'

Miranda thought quickly, 'She may be sickening for something My Lord, I would rather not risk bringing any sickness into the Palace.'

'Indeed, I will make sure that you have a maid to help you until your own is well again, the King would want nothing else' and with a smile that sent a strange feeling through Miranda he added, 'and neither would I'.

Within ten minutes Miranda found herself in a comfortable room, if Lord Benedict had been surprised that she had acquired a bag by the time he returned he had said nothing, just taken it from her and carried it as he escorted her and bade the maid look after her needs.

The wall hangings were of a gentle lilac, embroidered with woodland scenes, the rushes were fresh and sweet, it was too warm for a fire and the fireplace was heaped with fragrant dried flowers and herbs. The bed was large and high, the bedcurtains were drawn and the sheets were turned back showing spotless bedlinen.

The maid helped Miranda out of her gown and carefully laid aside her jewels. Miranda was thankful that the authenticity of the wardrobe department meant she was wearing a long white linen shift under the gown, no M&S lingerie to startle the maid. Part of Miranda's exhausted brain wondered what the equivalent of wearing clean underwear in case you got run over was at Henry's Court, maybe in case you got killed at the joust.

'This is a rare piece Mistress' said the maid admiringly looking at the bag. 'I have never seen the like of such work.' Miranda felt a pang of alarm, had she been careless even though she had removed the label of the bag? Was it all going to fall apart so soon?

The maid continued, 'Some visitors from foreign parts had something like but not as fine as this.'

Miranda relaxed a little, 'Thank you Betsy, yes, my father was much travelled and generous with his homecoming gifts.'

She smiled and Betsy shook out the dove grey day gown and pretty matching crescent hood edged with pearls ready for the morning, she then took Miranda's hair down from its fastenings and brushed it until it gleamed. As an unmarried woman Miranda could wear her hair loosely braided and with a hood that enhanced her beautiful honey and caramel hair, rather than hiding it.

'Will you be wanting some wine and honey cakes before bed Mistress?'

Miranda suddenly realised that she hadn't eaten since lunchtime and was ravenous. 'I am very hungry Betsy, that would be most welcome'

When Betsy returned she brought bread and cold meats as well and Miranda ate hungrily. Betsy poured warm water from the jug into the bowl and scents of chamomile and rosemary drifted into the room, she laid a soft washing cloth and a small piece of soap made with olive oil alongside the bowl, curtseyed to Miranda and left. Miranda soaped her tired body gently by soft candlelight, it wasn't a walk-in shower but it was delicious, the whole ritual soothed and quieted her racing mind.

She dried herself and dressed in the fresh linen shift from her bag, the floral scents from the fabric conditioner added to the beautiful scents that would forever mark this day in her memories.

Miranda sipped the delicious wine and ate the remaining honey cakes, for the first time that day she could let down her guard and think about what had happened. It had been no mistake that first time, the King was drawn to her, and what an intoxicating dance, so different from anything she had ever known. Lord Benedict had been wonderful too.

The wine and the events of the day combined to induce heavy sleepiness. Miranda looked under the bed with some trepidation, wondering what on earth she would do if the necessary pot was not there, it was, and had a secure lid, Miranda had no idea what would happen to the contents and she was too tired to worry about it.

It briefly crossed her mind that coming back to Henry's time as a chamber maid might not have held the same appeal. She climbed inside the lavender scented sheets and blew out the candle, she was asleep in seconds.

◆◆◆

Chapter 6
The morning walk

'Mistress, you must hurry!' 'Why, what's wrong?' Miranda awoke as Betsy rushed about opening curtains. hurriedly pouring fresh water into the basin and filling a small dish with leaves of mint and parsley for Miranda to chew as a mouth freshener.

'The King will be sending a gentleman of the Court to escort you to walk with him in the gardens, we have little time!'

'How do you know Betsy?' Miranda was wide awake now, splashing her face with the rose scented water and submitting to Betsy's urgent ministrations with the hairbrush, Betsy expertly styled Miranda's hair with the use of hairpins and the pretty crescent seed pearl hood that matched her dove grey gown.

'My sister's boy was taking in the water to Lord Benedict Marchant's chambers when the King's messenger arrived, Lord Benedict was fast asleep and he is making as much haste as he can to come to you.'

Miranda was thankful for the servants' underground network, even more so when Betsy produced a stomacher and proceeded to lace her into it. 'Mistress, I saw you had none, my dear mistress that I have looked after for many years has lately left the Court and retired to a quieter life of prayer and contemplation where she did not need me anymore, some things she left behind and said I may do with them as I think best.' Betsy laced and straightened as she talked, within a shorter time than seemed possible Miranda looked every inch the elegant lady who has quietly prepared herself for the coming day.

'You have been a blessing Betsy, thank you.'

Betsy hesitated, 'May I speak Mistress?'

'Of course, please do.'

'Since my mistress has gone I have been part of the general household, if your maid does not gain her health soon it would give me much pleasure to serve you.' Betsy's broad face was hopeful, it had been a severe loss of status in the servants' hierarchy to lose her place as Lady's maid to an inner member of the Court.

She could no longer look knowing when delicious gossip was being passed from ear to ear or enjoy the frantic rush when the King's pleasure or displeasure meant that servants raced across the Palace to win favour at different doors. For every living soul at the Palace, from Courtier to scullery maid, keeping Henry happy was paramount. The whole Court constantly felt the temperature of the words, looks and invitations that told how the breeze was blowing on any given day or hour. Sometimes the breeze was balmy and caressing, other times sharp and icy, either way, a good servant knew how to keep favour with well-timed information and a wise master or mistress knew when to listen.

The servants' grapevine was no less buzzing with Henry's interest in the new arrival at Court than was that of the Ladies in Waiting. The Queen's ladies were too wise to say a word in front of Anne of course but the abrupt silences and quick changes of subject told her everything she needed to know that morning.

Today the way the wind blew was in Miranda's favour and Betsy was determined to make the most of the good fortune that had sent Miranda into her life. 'Betsy, please do stay with me until my maid recovers her health, I cannot allow the possibility of bringing illness into the Palace. This is my first time at Court and I do not know its ways, I am sure you can help me greatly.'

Betsy was bursting with pride at how beautiful Miranda looked as she fastened a beautiful pearl necklace at her throat, it was the only genuine piece of jewelry Miranda had brought with her, it had been her mother's most treasured possession and had fortunately been passed to Miranda before her father had remarried. Whether her stage rubies and diamonds would pass muster she could not know, but she had no fears for her pearls.

Miranda welcomed Lord Benedict as graciously as if the frantic rush had never happened, she was amused to see that he too looked as calm and immaculately turned out in a deep russet doublet and hose as if he had risen several hours ago and walked through his morning most peacefully. He offered Miranda his arm and they set off together.

As they emerged from the Palace, the sight of the beautiful day and the perfect setting of the gardens alongside the waters of the Thames raised Miranda's spirits. Even though her heart was thundering at the potential prospect of being caught out, she was enjoying the morning. She tried to tell herself that it was because she was surely on the verge of writing the greatest thesis of all time but she spotted the King and his entourage in the distance and her heart gave a great thump of anticipation. Lord Benedict made kind enquiries of her health and remarked on the freshness of the morning, even though Miranda was too excited to fully take in what he was saying she knew that he was trying to put her at her ease and was grateful.

She swept into a low curtsey as they reached the King who had turned to give them a hearty welcome. Miranda felt a rush of happiness as the King offered her his arm, they began their walk through the immaculately tended gardens together and the King's entourage fell back to allow them to talk privately together.

'I have not forgotten my promise Mistress Miranda, only the most beautiful bloom in my gardens shall be sufficient to reflect your beauty, I will take you to my favourite place, a sheltered spot little known to many at Court.'

The King was dazzling, he was dressed magnificently in kingfisher blue shot through with silver thread. He had an aura about him, yes it was partly his power but it was more than that. To be on the receiving end of his full attention was to make Miranda feel as if she was the only person on earth who mattered or existed; to feel so fully present in the moment was almost shocking; to be fully aware of the blood tingling in her fingertips as her hand lay on Henry's arm; the very scents of the luxuriant and abundant honeysuckle seemed to weave into the moment, every sense was heightened.

'Thank you Your Majesty, you are very kind, I little imagined that I would be walking in your Majesty's gardens today, still less that my companion would do me so much honour.' The shy look Miranda gave him was not feigned, the boldness that had come courtesy of the mask at the ball was in retreat now.

'You are new to Court Mistress Miranda? I feel sure that I would recall if we had met before?' The King's penetrating blue eyes looked directly into hers, it was almost a form of hypnotism, the intensity of his gaze holding hers. 'I am My Lord, at home in Cumberland we have lived very quietly. My father was a scholarly man who had a love of languages and the plants and rare creatures of many lands. A lack of solitude was a trial for his gentle nature. I am not familiar with the ways of Court, I hope I will not make too many errors.'

Henry patted her hand on his arm, 'Indeed it is most refreshing to have you here, errors will always be forgiven, there could be no ill will coming from one such as you.' Miranda blushed, it was as natural as spring rainfall to feel warmed through by the King's attentions. 'And your father is no longer with you?'

'I had the sadness to lose him some months back My Lord, at the same time the fever took the man I had been betrothed to. I have no other close relations and I thought to ask at Court for a position if my learning in Latin and French could be of use in any way. I must confess Your Majesty that I was surprised to be expected to join the ball when I arrived and given a mask. I have been somewhat anxious in case it was all an error and I should not have been there'

Miranda almost held her breath as she waited to see if this would be accepted, could she really just walk into the Court of one of the most powerful men in the world in this way? But Henry was not as interested in her father and how she came to attend the dance as in her betrothed, 'You have my most heartfelt condolences for your losses Mistress Miranda, you were to have been married soon?'

Miranda hesitated, the King could see that she was choosing her words carefully, 'My betrothed was of very advanced years Your Majesty, my father thought that he would take care of me and I respected his wishes of course, the wedding was planned for this year and now sadly will never be.'

Henry smiled, there was no doubt that her heart had not been touched and she was not grieving for her betrothed. 'You need worry not about whether you are welcome at this

Court Mistress Miranda, you are here as my guest. Will you trust me to find you a position at my Court where your learning will be much valued?' 'With all my heart your Majesty! You do me such honour!'; Miranda's eyes shone and the King was pleased, he patted her hand upon his arm and pointed out some of the hidden beauties of his gardens. When they reached the sheltered spot the King had talked about he picked a single rosebud of a pink so delicate that it was almost white, totally out of sight of the retinue for a few precious moments he murmured, 'Miranda, a rose in waiting' and presented it to her, she took it silently, their fingers brushing, the slight touch sending unnerving sensations throughout both their bodies, his eyes never leaving her face.

◆◆◆

Chapter 7
A most welcome errand

Lord Benedict Marchant made a low bow to Miranda before offering his arm to escort her back to her apartment, he was solicitous when he learned that she had not yet broken her fast that morning. She realized that he must be in exactly the same situation as his hurried awakening and subsequent devotion to the King's wishes exactly echoed her own.

His intention to remedy the situation was not needed however as Betsy had ensured that spiced fruitcake and ale was waiting together with a glistening bowl of cherries, Miranda smiled ruefully as she thought of the huge baskets of cherries in the royal kitchens, she wondered if she had made it into the kitchen gossip yet, she somehow thought she probably had.

'Lord Benedict, I would like to send the King a gift to thank him for his kindness, would you be kind enough to give it to him please?'

'Nothing would give me more pleasure Mistress Miranda, it will be a most welcome errand.' Lord Benedict was curious, as far as he could tell the lady was without wealth or high birth, if she hadn't caught the King's eye at the ball there would be no place for her at Court, what could she be planning to give him? Others had risen from humble beginnings at the King's pleasure, look at Cromwell the blacksmith's son. Miranda was pleasing to the eye, spoke well and softly and danced with grace and elegance, if that was good enough for the King the Court had better make very sure it was good enough for them too. Lord Benedict caught himself in a wry grin as he thought of the Boleyns,

The Howards and the Seymours going along with this happy picture.

Miranda handed him a book tied with a pale green silk ribbon, he was intrigued. 'How came you by such vellum? It feels so rich beneath my hand.'

'My father was much travelled in his quest for knowledge Lord Benedict, I am fortunate that he was so generous to his only child. He had not great wealth but he had a learned mind and often spied treasures that were different to the treasures of other men.'

'And what message for his Majesty Mistress Miranda?' Lord Benedict was often the bearer of gifts to the King, he hoped for Miranda's sake that the gift would please, he knew well how quickly Henry's favour could be lost.

'Please tell him that this is a very humble gift, a poem I have written that I hope will please him.' Miranda was genuinely nervous, 'What do you think Lord Benedict? Do I presume too much to think that something I have written could please the King?'

Lord Benedict Marchant smiled, 'All will be well, a gift given with a good and loyal heart cannot but fail to please.'

****

Even George and Mary Boleyn who had withstood the worst of many such scenes, blanched at the fury that emanated from the stiff figure whose every nerve and sinew spoke of the fury that possessed her.

'Much travelled scholar!' the Queen spat the words, the venom distorting her face, Mary could not help thinking that 'The Most Happy' was not the most apt description of her sister at this moment.

'He pays attentions to the daughter of an inky fingered clerk who no doubt counts his master's beans on board ship! Why does he not take the scrubbing woman to bed and be done with it!'

Mary tried to soothe, 'be calm Anne, as you say she could not be less, she is a nobody from nowhere and cannot ever be a threat.'

'She is no threat! It is the insult to me that I cannot bear, I will not allow it!'

Anne was panting in her anger, it was disturbing to see. Mary knew that it was useless to try to calm her, this terrible passion would take her once again to the point where she angered the King, she could not see that her volatility no longer held charms for the man who would once have done anything to appease her.

The inevitable confrontation followed a path that all except Anne could have predicted, to hear the King say so coldly, 'Madam, do you presume to tell me whom I may or may not invite to my Court?' was painful to those who loved Anne but she could count very few friends now, too many had been treated carelessly or worse during her seemingly unstoppable rise.

The King strode away in the blackest of humours, he carried Miranda's book in his hand.

'Benedict! Where is your grandmother? Is she well?'

'She is at home in Wiltshire and is as well as can be expected for a lady of her years Your Majesty, her mind is as sharp as ever.' Lord Benedict bowed gracefully as he answered the King.

'And her tongue?' Henry calmed a little and gave a faint smile, Benedict was relieved to see that his grandmother was not the cause of the King's anger, Lady Marchant was known for her forthright views and she rarely held back on them for anyone. Fiercely loyal to the throne as she was it would be strange for her to have offended the King but not impossible.

Benedict gave a rueful smile, 'well……….',

'Say no more! You are a dutiful grandson I know!' Henry's mood could change like the sun emerging after a storm and this was one of those times.

'Would your grandmother like to join us at Court Benedict? It is a long time since I have had the pleasure of conversing with so fine a mind.'

Benedict was more than certain that his grandmother would not at all like to leave White Hart Manor in Wiltshire and come back to Court. She had found it painfully difficult to curtsey to Anne Boleyn. For her, Katherine was and always would be the anointed Queen. Fortunately, her advancing years had allowed her to claim the sanctuary of her manor, she may have a reputation for a sharp tongue but she was no fool, one slip and the future of Benedict and his sister would look very grim, these were not times to take foolish risks.

'My grandmother will be honoured to be invited Your Majesty and would take much pleasure in such stimulating conversation, I shall send a messenger immediately and make arrangements to ensure her comfort on the journey.'

'Excellent, and order the most comfortable of apartments for her use while she is here and your dear sister must come too! Benedict, I will want your grandmother to read this when she arrives.'

Benedict took the beautiful book, 'You may read it' said Henry.   There was silence while Benedict read and then re-read the poem, the King watched him keenly, 'Well?'

Benedict was genuinely amazed, 'This is no maid's love sonnet Your Grace!'

The King smiled, 'indeed it is not, now you see why I thought of Lady Marchant and her fierce intellect, I feel that this would be of great interest to her.'

'Your Majesty has a shrewd insight into what will intrigue my grandmother' Lord Benedict bowed low and took his leave to send a messenger with all haste and arrange an escort to bring his grandmother and sister to Court. He had done his very best to keep his dear Maria from the Court for as long as possible, citing her devotion to her grandmother's needs.

He wondered what else the King wanted of his grandmother, not only to discuss poetry if he knew the King. But what poetry! He felt stirred by reading it as if for a joust or a battle, some of the lines had struck such a chord with him and they kept repeating in his mind, he knew that he had risked it all on one game of pitch and toss and may well have to start again at his beginnings. He could deal with that, what he couldn't deal with was having put his grandmother and Maria in the same position too. His worries overshadowed even being called upon to serve his King and involve his grandmother and sister.

Miranda paced her room anxiously, what if the poem was considered outrageous? Plagiarism would be the least of her worries if she offended the King, she could hardly ask an armed guard to escort her to the dungeons via the alcove, she felt that the key was safely at her neck, what if things went wrong and she never returned to her own time? Poor

Alice wouldn't know what to do, there was no family member she could call.

She started at the knock at the door, 'Lord Benedict!'

He grinned, suddenly looking as young as he really was, 'The King is most intrigued by your poem, I feel sure he will want to discuss it further with you'

Relief flooded through Miranda, 'Intrigued in a good way?' As she spoke the words she realized that the phrase was from a different time but Lord Benedict seemed to enjoy it,

'Yes, Intrigued in a good way! And may I say Mistress Miranda…' Benedict hesitated, his charming Court manners deserted him for a moment, he felt almost shy, a feeling little known to a man who was so sought after by women, 'The King let me read it, I cannot describe the storm of feeling it aroused in me, such talent and unlike anything I have ever read before by maid or man.'

◆◆◆

Chapter 8

Lady Marchant

'Bring my grandson to me.' Lady Marchant's order was a little less imperious than normal, this was the only hint that she had travelled for three hours in dust and heat. Her servants, who had of course travelled with her, busied themselves making sure that wine was brought, rose water poured into the washing basin, and a small perfectly circular cheese with plum and apple chutney appeared from a traveling basket to tempt her appetite.

Lady Marchant, leaned back and closed her eyes for a moment, it seemed that she was to be brought back onto the Palace stage again, no doubt she would soon know why. Lady Maria was at her grandmother's side in an instant, applying cooling rosewater to her wrists and quietly handing her the wine goblet. Moments later Lady Marchant was as straight backed and gracious as ever, her Courtier's demeanour back in place as easily as slipping on a much worn favourite cloak that had lain forgotten for four full seasons.

'Grandmother! How came you to make such haste? I did not expect you could reach Court until tomorrow or even later.' Benedict kissed his grandmother's hand as he spoke and then hugged his sister, at fourteen she was becoming a beauty.

'Your messenger was met with the news that we were visiting only hours away from the palace, being a sensible lad he came straight to us and we were able to set off early this morning.'

'Grandmother! you did not tell me that you were away from home, I could have arranged for your comfort while you travelled. Maria, why did you not send word to me?'

'Benedict, when the day comes when I cannot arrange a short visit without your help you may order your mourning clothes with all haste.' Lady Marchant firmly believed that she was more than capable of riding at the head of an advancing army if the need arose, two husbands had hardly dampened her indomitable spirit, age was the only enemy that was creeping up on her defences but even that battle would not be quietly surrendered.

Maria gave a shrug and a 'what can I do?' look at Benedict, he smiled back. Lord Benedict had the command of a thousand men and had gained their respect from the very first time he was tried in battle but he knew better than to try to overrule his grandmother.

Lady Marchant dismissed the servants, 'Now what's this all about? Why has the King summoned me? Out with it now Benedict, you must not allow me to enter the jousts unarmed.'

Benedict glanced towards his sister, 'I am not sure it is a suitable discussion for Maria.' 'Nonsense. Maria is of marriageable age, if this summons is regarding a husband for her she must face it as stalwartly as I did at her age.'

'It is not that Grandmother'. Benedict was gentle, he knew that his grandmother considered the Court a dangerous place these days, behind her brave words was a heart troubled by what may be coming. 'It is of another lady we will speak.'

'Maria can stay, she must learn of the world even though I would keep her from it for a few years more.'

Silently Benedict handed his grandmother the book, a thing of beauty in itself, she opened it and read it thoroughly, like her grandson she read it twice before looking up. 'Remarkable, I take it we have a new poet, how does Lord Thomas Wyatt think on that?'

Lord Benedict smiled, his grandmother was a born politician, not five minutes arrived and already moving the chess pieces of favour and ambition around the chequered board of Henry's entourage in her mind. 'This was written by a Mistress Miranda Glover, she is currently at Court and has caught the eye of the King. He thought that you would be interested in such a talent'

'This must be a remarkable young lady'

'She is…refreshing, and… I like her.'

Lady Marchant looked up, suddenly alert and wary, 'I am no fool Grandmother' Benedict spoke quietly, there was understanding between them.

'So why am I here? It is true I am interested in such a mind that could create this but this is not why the King has brought me.'

'You are correct Grandmother, he has not confided in me but I believe that he would like the young lady to stay at Court and she has no friends or relatives here.'

'No friends or relatives at Court? Then who is she?'

'She is the daughter of a humble man, now dead, he was a learned man I believe and encouraged learning in his daughter, there is no wealth or status in the family.'

'Mistress Miranda Glover must have very special charms indeed! But Benedict, she will be eaten alive here, the fury of the Howards and Seymours will be boundless. Why on earth does he not house her nearby where he can visit her discreetly?'

'I believe that Anne Boleyn ordered him to send her away, so now he shows the Queen that he cannot be ordered, the tide is turning but she will not heed it. As to Mistress Miranda being eaten alive, I believe that may be where your help may be called upon Grandmother.'

Lady Marchant glanced at Maria, 'Close your mouth Maria! You will hear more than this before this visit is ended. Serenity of expression is always wise.' Maria closed her mouth abruptly, to think that she might have missed this! The quiet charms of Wiltshire were not so appealing to a young girl who longed for some excitement.

By the time the King did Lady Marchant the unexpected honour of visiting her apartments to welcome her back to Court, she was ready with her deepest curtsey and most welcoming expression.

'My dearest Lady Marchant! What a pleasure to see you once again at Court! How do you like to be back?'

'I like it very much Your Majesty, you do me and my Granddaughter much honour with your kind invitation. May I present Lady Maria? This is her first visit to your Court.'

The King bade Lady Maria most welcome, at a nod from Lady Marchant, her servants and Maria withdrew and left her alone with the King. Lady Marchant wasted no time, 'Your Majesty, my grandson has shown me the Poem IF…, I would know the Lady who has such a mind, I do not know when I have ever read anything such as this.'

'I cannot tell you how much it pleases me to hear you say this Lady Marchant, I would keep such a rare talent with us for a little while. Mistress Miranda Glover is new to Court and has no friends or family here. She is of humble birth, this will surprise you when you meet her as her natural elegance and gentle manners are most fitting.'

'Your Majesty, if it pleases you I would like to invite Miss Glover to stay in my apartments, that would give me the opportunity to talk with her and I can be useful in showing her the ways of Court. She will be company for Lady Maria too. Does she play and sing?'

'That I do not know Lady Marchant, it would be most pleasant to hear singing in my apartments before we dine this evening.'

'Your Majesty, I will ensure that you have the pleasure of song this evening, I will bring Mistress Miranda and Lady Maria to visit and I am sure that Lord Benedict will escort us; if I do not find at least one songbird for you I will be very surprised.'

The King's mood was light as he left and as soon as he had gone Lady Marchant's servants set to work. Within two hours Miranda had been moved lock, stock and barrel to a beautiful room in Lady Marchant's apartments. Betsy was tenaciously holding on to her new post, insisting on taking charge of unpacking and arranging Miranda's few possessions, being careful not to mention that she wasn't Miranda's normal maid. She needn't have worried; Lady Marchant's servants weren't looking for any additional duties.

Miranda's tete a tete with Lady Marchant didn't get off to a good start, after a gracious welcome Miranda told her story of accidentally ending up at the ball, Lady Marchant did an excellent impression of a kindly elderly lady while she listened.

'Have you quite finished?'

Miranda was a little disconcerted by the gimlet stare, 'er yes Your Ladyship.'

'I find it so odd that younger people should try and patronise their elders, do you really think that those who are some years in advance of you will be taken in by such obvious, and frankly, pathetic lies? Do you really think that we haven't also plotted and used our many and varied charms in our youth to jump over people's heads? Do you think that women haven't always used their influence to get what they want? What do you think happens? that when we reach the age where the plump and pretty cheek loses a little of its softness that we suddenly forget how all this is done? People would sell their kin to get an invitation to a royal ball, nobodies do NOT just walk in and accidentally get directed to join the dance. Now, start again and King or no King you will be dismissed from my chambers if I don't hear the ring of truth in your tale.'

Miranda's wine goblet shook in her hand, it was like being interrogated by a High Court Judge you had mistaken for a sweet old lady selling jam at a village fete. Miranda had yet to learn that she had a lot to learn.

She took a deep breath and started again. 'I am from a very humble background My Lady, I had an old friend amongst the Palace Servants and I asked them to help me meet the King, I confess that I believed that if we met I could win his interest. I have long dreamt of living a different life, if I was a man I would have tried my chance in battle, instead I use different weapons in my quest,'

Lady Marchant nodded, 'Better, who is this friend?'

'I will never say My Lady, if you want me to leave Court and never return then I will but I will never tell you who helped me find my way to the King's ball.'

'Good, loyalty is an excellent quality, although do not believe for one moment that you wouldn't betray your friend if the King decided that there had been treasonous behaviour' said Lady Marchant approvingly. 'So, what are your ambitions? What do you want from this? No nonsense now, let us understand one another.'

'I would like the King to admire me, I have such love and loyalty in my heart for him.'

Lady Marchant looked at her steadily 'and?'

People of all sorts of noble heritage had quailed before Lady Marchant's stare, Miranda was no match for her, 'If the King's notice could help me live a little less humbly I would be grateful.'

'And find you a good husband when your time in the sun is over?' No-one could accuse Lady Marchant of short term thinking. Miranda realised that Janet the bulldozer faded into insignificance when held up to the light against the real thing.

'Indeed no!' Miranda burst out, 'I'd like to have enough wealth to live as I please!'

Lady Marchant laughed aloud, 'I think that we are hearing the truth now indeed. Believe me, living as you please comes after many years of paying your dues as a wife if you're lucky enough to outlive a husband or two. You won't escape the marriage bed my dear, whether you get a well feathered one will depend on how much you please the King and how graciously you accept the farewell when it comes.'

Miranda's head felt as if it would explode with all the tightropes she was walking, here she was, an independent woman of the twenty first century talking about marriage as the only career option, indeed, talking about being the King's mistress as a career option!

What if she never got back? What if this did indeed become her life? What if she didn't get back for work tomorrow? What if the people around the King made more determined efforts to investigate her background? The most her stepmother and the bulldozer could do was keep her short of money, Henry VIII had chopped off the heads of two of his wives! Although he didn't know that yet of course.

She wanted to see him again, this disturbing man with an animal magnetism that eclipsed even his power as King. At this point in time he was not the monster that history had subsequently painted him, overshadowing the years where he was the favourite of the Court and the people and reigned with the wise and guiding hand of Katherine, Princess of the blood, beside him. Miranda could not help her mind going a little way down a path where the meeting with Miranda diverted the known flow of history.

Lady Marchant brought her out of her reverie, 'The King likes you. I will help you navigate the traps and pitfalls of the Court. Both you and I will make sworn enemies of Anne Boleyn and the many others who will be sorely tried to see you best those who jostle to be close to the King. Never underestimate those who would act against you, this is no game, the stakes are high and the losing can be fatal. But, if you can keep the King happy for the summer you will reap rewards, if you can keep him happy for longer you may well benefit your line for generations to come. The King is immensely generous to his favourites. Now to your poetry, speak now, did your father write it?'

'No indeed Madam, he did not!' This at least was a firm truth.

'I am pleased to hear it. Do you play and sing?' 'I do My Lady, but I would be nervous to play when I was not familiar with the instrument. I have no music with me.' This was a tight spot, what was the name of the keyboard instrument like a piano? How could she play it? There was no chance of being able to sing any of the songs.

'Lady Maria has music and will practice with you, she will accompany your singing on the virginal, it will be a most charming tableau for the King.'

To Miranda's immense relief Lady Marchant dismissed her to spend time with Lady Maria to practice. Maria was disappointed to realise that Miranda knew even less Court gossip than she did but this was more than made up for by the fact that they were all going to the King's private apartments! Maria could hardly believe that only yesterday she had been living the quietest of lives and now she was in the thick of it. They played and sang a beautiful composition called, 'Pastimes with good company', it had to performed to perfection, not least because it had been composed by the King. Miranda gave silent thanks that she had studied Latin and medieval French. She also watched Lady Maria carefully as she played the virginal and eventually felt confident enough to ask if she could try. It was a fascinating instrument and a highly proficient piano player like Miranda could find her way around it, it would need hours of practice for her to feel confident though.

Lady Maria clapped her hands when her grandmother told her it was time to look out her prettiest gown, 'What a day Grandmother! If only Benedict's worries could find solace too I cannot imagine how anyone could be happier!'

Miranda looked enquiringly at Lady Marchant who said, 'it is not a secret although we do not trouble our friends with it.'

Maria blushed as her grandmother glanced at her. 'Too much of our family fortune is invested in Benedict's ships that have not been heard from these many months. If The Elizabeth Marchant and The White Hart do not come home, then things will go hard with the Marchants.'

◆◆◆

Chapter 9
The musical evening

Betsy had lost no time in letting the most senior of Lady Marchant's servants know that it would be most useful to be able to purchase some enhancements for Miranda's wardrobe. This information was dealt with speedily and a line of credit was arranged to ensure that the finest trimmings would be delivered immediately and that new gowns could be ordered. Betsy's position in the servants' hierarchy was nicely restored and she set to with a will. If her lady didn't outshine every other this evening it wouldn't be for want of Betsy's efforts. If Betsy could have seen the King's face as Miranda followed Lady Marchant into his presence she would have felt herself well rewarded. He greeted Lady Marchant, Lord Benedict and Lady Maria with much pleasure and enquired kindly for their comfort at Court but when he turned to Miranda there was a perceptible softening of his face, his look had the same eagerness as a young boy, his voice was gentle and he took Miranda's hand to raise her from her curtsey. Miranda felt the blood pulse into her fingertips, her whole body seemed drawn towards the King, no matter where she looked her eyes were drawn back to him. Miranda felt grateful to Lady Marchant for keeping up the conversation, she wasn't sure that she could add anything coherent never mind amusing. Lady Marchant asked Henry if it would be his pleasure to hear some music and singing and as Miranda moved to the virginal with Maria she thought that everyone must surely see her hands shaking. Then Maria started playing and the music flooded Miranda's very being, soothed her soul and heightened her experience of being in the world, she felt the notes rather than heard them and her singing silenced the room. Neither Henry nor Benedict could take their eyes from her face. They finished their song to much praise, the King was much pleased at how beautifully they had brought his composition to life, his love of music was perhaps the best part of his character and this was the side he showed now. As a handsome young page rushed to help a gently blushing Maria with her music sheets, Henry gave Miranda his arm and they withdrew to sit in a secluded window seat. Many people would have liked to know what was said, but only if they had composed and brought song to life from the inner well of creativity could they have understood it. It was a meeting of souls; on that evening at Greenwich Palace two people forged a bond that was outside the common experience of either of them. They both knew that their simmering attraction would come to be the first thing with them again, but not tonight. The yearning in Miranda's heart was reflected in Henry's, for her part she felt a rush of acute sadness to know that his coming years would be blighted by the damage yet to be done to his poor leg; for his part he felt a tenderness that cracked a little of the hardened shell that he had grown to survive in his world. He knew the fleeting wish to be ordinary, to walk his love along the riverbank in the warm summer air and have no battalions of Kings, Popes and Dukes lining up to pass judgement on his conduct. When he had lost Katherine, he had lost the steadfast love that treasured him at all times, his own fault yes, but a loss nevertheless. Without being able to name it, his heart sought that constancy again after the turbulent years with Anne.

Miranda promised to play and sing some music of her own composition next time they met, Henry said that he would like that above all things, he covered her hand gently with his own, a small movement unobserved by the rest of the company.

Later, when they had returned to their own welcoming and comfortable apartments to sip a little warmed wine, Lady Marchant looked at her two grandchildren and Miranda and realised that every single one of them looked dazed with love. Thank goodness someone in the family was able to keep a level head, they had no idea of the storms ahead.

Possibly the most triumphant was Betsy, as she helped a sleepy Miranda off with her gown and pearls she couldn't help running a few, 'It's wouldn't be right for me to say' scenarios in her head for the following day . Miranda's star was rising and Betsy was going up too, even if she had to hang on to the hem of Miranda's gown with her fingertips.

◆◆◆

Chapter 10

The morning after

Miranda's heart was heavy as she quietly and carefully placed each item in her bag in the silence of the dawn. She felt a pang of affection for Betsy as sprigs of lavender fell to the floor from her beautifully laundered shift. It was so comforting to be looked after again, between Lady Marchant and Betsy she felt mothered for the first time in many years. Both Betsy and Lady Marchant would have been astonished to think of themselves in that light, but Miranda was coming first with someone for the first time in many years, it was a good feeling.

She stepped carefully outside the door, no-one was yet stirring and she reached the alcove in the Great Hall passing only sleeping servants.

As the whirling sensation passed, Miranda moved quietly through the film set, deserted at the moment but that wouldn't last long, the technicians would be arriving by six. She needed to have returned the gowns to wardrobe and changed before anyone arrived. As soon as the doors were opened by the first to arrive she would be able to slip outside unseen and return at her call time. No time to get home first though.

Within an hour she was sipping a coffee and enjoying a cheese and tomato toasted sandwich at a nearby cafe. There were 6 texts and a missed call from Alice on her phone. Miranda messaged her straight away, she didn't feel up to a call, there was too much she needed to think through first.

'Hi, nightmare, phone was lost down the side of the sofa! going straight to work, see you tonight.'

'Glad you're OK, meet anyone nice?'

'You have a totally one track mind Alice!'

'Hmm, not a denial though!'

Miranda wondered what Alice would do if she really gave her all the details, she would hardly be able to believe her unless she saw it all with her own eyes. Would other people be able to go through the door? She had taken objects through with no problems and she had inadvertently brought some sprigs of lavender back with her but what about people? Could she ever take that level of responsibility? It really wasn't a game, fall foul of the people with power in Henry's Court and the outcome didn't bear thinking about. She had also left the vellum book in Henry's time, what of that now?

Miranda was having difficulty remembering that her main ambition was meant to be getting unique material for her thesis, Henry's gentle covering of her hand was like a physical memory being re-lived over and over in her body.

After a day of mostly waiting about on the film set, Miranda was glad to head home. She arrived an hour before Alice and had time to surprise her by cooking a delicious penne arrabiata, they didn't always cook for each other but now and then it was nice to come home to supper.

'I will be literally five minutes, no objections if you want to open the wine!' Alice was as good as her word, within five minutes flat she had shed her suit, shoes and make up and re-appeared in her pyjamas. She gave a huge sigh of satisfaction as Miranda opened the oven and took out the garlic bread, she put it on the table alongside the pasta dish and the bowl of salad.

Alice's funny stories of the day at work took Miranda out of herself for the first time in days, it was an immense relief to be able to fully let her guard down and just be herself for a few hours.

Miranda was so tired, she had never been so grateful for the absolute luxury of a deep foamy bath and luxuriated in the blended scents of lavender and almond. The present time had so many everyday blessings, so many things that she had completely taken for granted. Every single thing in the bathroom was seen in a new light. The thought that she could just step into the shower in the morning was her last drifting image as the pleasure of sleeping in her own bed sent her quickly into a deeply refreshing sleep.

◆◆◆

Chapter 11
The butterfly's wing

Miranda started the next day with her cool researcher's brain fired up and ready to go. The wonderful shower was followed up with a brisk walk to get the day started. Even though she wouldn't get paid she was still glad that she wasn't needed on set today, they would be doing close ups with the main characters and most of the extras had the day off. Normally she would have called the agency to see if there was anything else going but there was a lot she needed to do.

She created a folder and a list of all she wanted to research, she would add to it as she went but there was too much flying around in her head to try and do it without some sort of structure. She decided to try to identify the exact time of her visits to Henry's Court first and then to try and find out whether there was anything at all about Lord Benedict and his ships in history.

She set up files for these areas and then added another for Time Travel, there must be something out there if others had experienced it.

Miranda was still in maximum efficiency mode when she opened up one of the most serious academic websites on Henry VIII, the images of his six wives were still looking out at her but within the first few lines of text she was brought to an absolute standstill. The words were unmistakable, 'Author of Britain's best loved poem IF' (disputed). Miranda's hand was shaking as she clicked on the link, it seemed that some academics believed that it must have been written by Lord Thomas Wyatt, the official Court poet. All academics agreed that it was a complete shift in the canon of literature whoever had written it. Miranda clicked on the link to the full poem and read, 'IF you can keep your calm when all about you are losing theirs and blaming it on you'

Miranda struggled to catch her breath, it was her version! History had been changed!

These thoughts were quickly followed by the realization that she didn't have history's recognition for it and then the thought that neither had the real poet Rudyard Kipling! She had to see what damage she had done to Kipling, she went straight to his Wiki page. Thank goodness, he had still written Jungle Book and all his other titles, he had still received the Nobel Prize for Literature, he was still considered to be a genius and a controversial character. She had stolen his poem but she hadn't destroyed his life.

But what did it all mean? Miranda had been sure that time had reset whenever she went back to Henry's time, how could this have happened? Everything went around and round in her head, there was no-one she could use as a sounding board.

She scribbled down competing thoughts, eventually she had three possible threads, the first was that time only reset when she went back to Henry's time, when she came back to her own time things continued in 1535, they did not reset. The second possibility was that things had changed because she had left a physical object from another time there; and lastly the most difficult thought to come to terms with was that maybe there were multiple realities, multiple tunnels of time running along similar but not identical tracks. This was all a bit worrying, had she inadvertently left Betsy and the Marchants to try and explain her disappearance to an angry King?

Miranda's disciplined plan gave way to a scattered delve into what people were saying about time travel on the internet, there were some people that just seemed very odd indeed and the online commenters were lining up to tell them exactly that. Miranda was very aware that she would become a fully paid up member of this group if she wasn't very careful about what she said about her experiences. She remembered her Mum saying firmly, 'there's only one way to keep a secret, tell no-one' when Miranda had tried to get some inside information on high profile events her Mum was organising. Right now this seemed like particularly good advice.

Then she hit on a rich seam of information surrounding two women who had written of something similar to her own experience at a Chateau in France. There were claims it was all fabricated and competing claims for its authenticity. The two women were serious academics, they had risked a great deal of derision to tell their story. Miranda felt her pulse rate speed up.

Next, she turned to the current scientific theories and made an amazing discovery. Hugely respected scientists were putting their heads above the parapet and saying that theoretical physics showed that time travel could not be ruled out! Even Stephen Hawking said it in a wonderful lecture that talked about cosmic strings and warped time; the essay itself was so beautiful that the words were magical even to a non-scientist. To make real sense of it Miranda would have to read it as a research project, investigating every sentence and word she didn't understand, for now, knowing that scientists were not ruling out the possibilities was enough.

There was a great deal to read up on and it was hard to pick out the wheat from the chaff, it was sobering to realise that she would probably have dismissed every one of these people telling their tales of time travel as fantasists or sadly deluded a few short weeks ago.

Miranda made herself a cup of tea to give herself a short break from the screen and then started to research Benedict and his lost ships. White Hart Manor in Wiltshire still existed, the family who lived there were very proud of the fact that they had lived there since the late 1500s, there was a small footnote saying that the beautiful manor had been originally designed and built by Lord William Marchant but that was all. The original history of the house and family had been overshadowed by those who came later. Miranda felt a deep pang of sympathy for Lady Marchant who loved it so deeply and for Maria and Benedict who may have been the people who had to part with their home.

The photographs were stunning, the house was impossibly elegant, the architecture simple, gracious and welcoming. The photographs of the interior showed beautifully proportioned rooms, flooded with sunlight, the main reception rooms all with French windows that led out onto the balustrade. The upstairs gallery, softly glowing with centuries old walnut and polished oak, was inset with huge doors leading off to the bedrooms. The bedroom windows looked out onto formal gardens and the maze at the front of the manor. The view from the rear facing rooms included wildflower areas, apple and plum trees and an enormous soft fruit and kitchen garden area.   The parkland that surrounded the acres nearest to the house gave onto a private woodland and the photographs showed it when the bluebells were in full bloom.

It was breathtaking, no wonder Lady Marchant longed for it after the cut and thrust of the Court. How could such a magnificent manor house still give the feeling it was a home?

A quote from the current owner said that, 'Our family has been here forever'. Not quite, thought Miranda and hoped fervently that Lady Marchant had ended her days as Mistress of her beloved home.

Miranda could find nothing at all on The Elizabeth Marchant, whether Benedict's ship had ever come home or not, history had no record of it ever existing. She struck gold within minutes of starting her search for The White Hart, it was well known amongst the people who followed these things.

The shipwreck had been discovered lodged in a seabed cleft off the coast of Sheerness in 1975. Salvage expeditions had yielded a treasure trove of gold and some of the largest rubies in known existence. There was a great deal of evidence to show that the ship had already been looted, the marine archeologists surmised that they had found the ship approximately forty years after it had first been disturbed. It seemed that the ship may have been visited over a period of many years before its solitude and silence were temporarily restored until the official find in 1975.

The fact that no-one had been aware of the plundering of the shipwreck showed that someone had really known how to keep a secret, to have dived in the same place over many years without drawing attention to themselves was quite something. Maybe they had thought there was no more to take or maybe their death had brought matters to an end; who knew what other amazing finds had been lost to the nation.

Remains of some of the original crew were found in the wreck. Knowing that Benedict would have counted friends amongst these people made it a sad read, far removed from an academic understanding of the facts. The marine archeologists had investigated all aspects of the shipwreck and surrounding seabed together with ancient shipping records and reached agreement that the closest they could date the ship being lost was the spring of 1535.

Miranda was overcome with sadness as she realised that while she had been talking to Benedict his ship was already lost and had been at the bottom of the silent ocean for many months. All the hopes of the family and of the families of the crew were for nothing, how long had they waited to see if their sons and husbands came home before they gave up on them? Benedict seemed to have hung on to White Hart Manor for at least ten more years, they must have been times of great struggle.

At that moment any lingering doubts about going back through the door were over. One way or another she was going to tell Benedict how to find his ship, the co-ordinates and the full description of where the ship lay were there for all to see and Miranda copied the information into her file. She stretched her aching back, too much computer today, she needed a long walk to clear her head and then check and recheck every detail again.

◆◆◆

Chapter 12

A risky business

Miranda's preparations were very detailed this time, she intended to stay for two weeks and this meant careful planning for two dimensions of time. The practicalities needed to be thought through and keeping a cool head to do this was a welcome distraction from the maelstrom of emotion that would overtake her at the oddest times.

Over and over she felt Henry's hand covering hers, gently capturing her whole heart in that moment. Again and again she re-lived that first dance where she had captivated the King but had the same spell had captured her own heart just as irrevocably? Over and over she heard Henry murmur, 'Miranda, a rose in waiting' Overwhelming yearning attraction and the feeling of souls meeting was a potent combination. Miranda was helpless when the feeling hit her, she felt as if she wanted to melt into Henry, to lean into his strength and protection.

At the same time she felt a protective urge towards him that seemed to have no reason, what protection could she offer to one of the most powerful Kings of all time? But as much as he was surrounded by people, she felt his loneliness; as much as he was all powerful she knew that his fine physical strength would come to be lost which would break his heart; as much as he could have any woman he wanted they all came with families hungry for advantage.

The most wonderful thing was that she could experience these things again, if she was careful not to set any other paths in motion she could once again dance with Henry, sing for him and walk with him in the gardens. It was a little like thinking about re-reading a much-loved book, you already know the pleasure it had brought before and this time there may be things you hadn't noticed, additional joys to be found.

The extras' work had one more week to run, the filming would continue for a few weeks after that. She would just have to hope that in all the confusion no-one noticed that she hadn't handed her costume back in, especially as she intended to borrow an additional gown and shift as before, this time she would also take an additional pair of the beautifully embroidered shoes. The other big danger was that her normal clothes and bag would be found before she came back, she certainly didn't want to be reported as a missing person.

One of the on-line time travelling claims had come about because a man had been charged with insider dealing on the stock exchange, unerringly picking out shares that soared in value, his defence had been that he had been travelling in time and knew which shares would do well. Just weeks ago Miranda would have thought this as hilarious as everyone else who roundly mocked him online; today, not so much at all. It crossed Miranda's mind that she could ensure her own financial future like this in some way. Too much to think about, first she would ensure that Lord Benedict's fortunes were restored and she could have her time with the King, that was more than enough to be juggling for now.

She ordered another vellum book of IF- with the one word change and then set to work to decide which pieces of music to take to play for Henry. She thought about her favourite poem, written by a contemporary poet, one that had helped when she had faced difficult times in her life.

If you painted your life

If you painted your life, would it mostly be grey?

With rare flames of scarlet for each special day
And the odd strand of silver where you kept your illusions
Mixed in with the blues marking times of confusion

If you painted your life would there be storms
For the times that you gave up and agreed to conform?
Perhaps you'd paint stars, one for each dream
That gave life a meaning or so it once seemed

Has anyone else painted clouds in your sky
And dulled your bright colours as your chances passed by?
Maybe it's time to take back the brush
Start painting your own life, enough is enough

You can paint rainbows, banishing grey
And splash on some gold, starting today
Puddles of silver; shimmering bright
Walk out of the shadows, come into the light.

Perhaps you need mellow, golden nut brown
Are you running too fast, is it time to slow down?
Paint yourself peace and space just to be
Gentle blue mornings, a soft lilac sea.

In your painting of life, let the beautiful days

Shimmer in gold and light up the greys

Paint it with courage, thread golden strands.

Pick up your brush, life's in your own hands.

By Beverley Williams

Miranda had written music to accompany this beautiful piece and it touched her heart when she played it. With practice, she thought she could play and sing 'If you painted your life' on the virginal, if she couldn't get to grips with it she could ask Maria to play if she took the music back with her.

She would need the music written up exactly as it would have been for 1535, again she could ask the specialist printer, giving a play or film as the reason if any queries came up. Her money was running out fast, at least the gorgeous Tudor tapestry bag didn't have to be paid for a second time.

She wanted to feel Henry's admiration again, wanting to please him was addictive. It was so wonderful to know that he desired her, to have the King of England tremble when he leaned forward to inhale the honeysuckle and lemon fragrance of her warm skin. She wanted to draw him to her with her songs, bind him tighter with the sweetest of harmonies and lyrics that would tell a little of what was in her heart.

After a little hesitation she added John Denver's sublime 'Annie's Song' to the printer's list, feeling more than a hint of sacrilege as she changed the title to 'A Lady's song for her husband' as she thought it best not to risk even a hint of scandal when singing as an unmarried lady.

The lyrics and music were so beautiful, they reached a place that couldn't be touched in everyday life. Miranda tried to remember when she had first heard the song, tried to imagine how Henry would react when he heard it, she knew he would remember the moment for the rest of his life. As Miranda thought about playing and singing the song for the King, she had a delightful vision of modestly meeting Henry's eyes as she sang so that he would know that the words were for him. It was so perfect, she wondered if Henry would ask her to come and play it to him when they were completely alone, there would be no going back if he did.

When the right time came, she would go through the door in the secret alcove at Greenwich and immediately come back again to reset everything that had been changed. Knowing that the poets and songwriters would still be inspired many centuries later, Miranda could find a way for her conscience to come to terms with the terrifying audacity of pretending that she had written these pieces. How she was going to do this while still helping Lord Benedict defeated her at the moment, it was all starting to feel like a massive equation sprawled over three whiteboards in a lecture theatre.

Miranda called the Supporting Artiste's Agency and told them she would be on holiday for two weeks when this assignment ended. Alice was frankly astounded when Miranda told her that she was going to go on a silent retreat in Devon for two weeks. Things were ready this side of time.

◆◆◆

Chapter 13
Mary Boleyn

Miranda couldn't remember when she had felt such happiness, she had been able to experience the excitement and overwhelming feelings of love once again as they danced and walked in the gardens, to see Henry's happiness when he talked to her and his longing for her in his beautiful blue eyes when she sang for him.

She had done her best to avoid annoying Lady Marchant on her first meeting but Lady Marchant's ability to sense an untruth had led to a very similar spiky exchange and eventual understanding.

Now, sitting with Lady Marchant and Lady Maria the morning after singing for the King, she thought again about how to give Lord Benedict the information he needed. How could she tell him where his ship was so that he could save his fortune and help the families of the men who were never coming home again? Miranda had absolutely no doubts he would do this, even though she had known Lord Benedict and his grandmother such a short time, the calibre of their character was unmistakable.

The man himself arrived at his grandmother's apartments, as if conjured up by Miranda's thinking of him. He kissed his grandmother and sister and bowed low to Miranda, including her in the warmth of his family greeting.

'The King enquires for your good health Grandmother and asks if you would like to join his party to watch the jousting today, his kind invitation includes my sister and Mistress Miranda, it would please him greatly to have your company.'

'Please tell his Majesty that we would be delighted to join him and thank him for his kindness. How is our dear Queen's health today?' Miranda marveled at the code being used, no spying servant could have faulted the conversation.

'The Queen is a little unwell today and will be resting. Some of her ladies will stay with her to ensure she has every comfort.' Lady Marchant understood full well that this meant that Anne's temper was unabated but that the coast was clear. Heaven only knew what heights of fury would be reached when she found out that Miranda had joined the King at the joust.

Lady Marchant knew that her own position as a matriarch of the Court and her family's position as loved friend and supporter of the King would only protect her as long as she had the King's protection. If the King lost interest in Miranda or Anne managed to turn him against her then nothing would save them all from the inevitable downfall. Wolsey's dreadful fall from favour when Anne took her revenge was a terrible warning to all who dared cross her. Yet, who could say no when the King asked something of them? Everyone at Court walked a difficult path, Lady Marchant was a seasoned courtier but these were no ordinary times.

'And will you join us Lord Benedict?' asked Miranda. 'I shall be taking part in the jousts Mistress Miranda, hopefully I will not join you too soon as that would mean I was one of the first unseated.' Lord Benedict smiled, 'but when my luck runs out I shall come to my grandmother for congratulations or solace.'

At that moment there was a flurry as Lady Mary, Anne Boleyn's sister entered, she curtseyed most prettily to Lady Marchant and smiled a golden sweet as honey smile encompassing all present. 'How wonderful to see you back at Court Lady Marchant, my sister the Queen sends you her good wishes and looks forward to your company in her apartments in a day or two when her health is a little better.' The sweetness never faltered for a second.

'Her Majesty's kindness does me much honour Lady Mary, nothing would give me greater pleasure. May I introduce my granddaughter Lady Maria and Mistress Miranda Glover? It is the first time at Court for them both.'

Lady Mary exchanged some kind words with Lady Maria, making her blush with happiness by telling her what a favourite her brother was at Court and how many young ladies would be hoping he might ask them for their favour to wear at the jousting today. 'Sadly, I shall have to disappoint them all Lady Mary, my grandmother has given me her favour and I shall be carrying the ivory and burgundy of the Marchant family today. I shall try and do honour to the memory of my father although I fear I can never live up to his reputation on the jousting field.'

'Never doubt that he would have been proud of you Benedict, as are we all.' Lady Marchant's imperious voice softened a little as she thought of her son, lost in Henry's service on the battlefield, courageous in death as he was in life.

Miranda tried to control her nerves, there was only one reason that Mary had turned up. All of Miranda's research had led her to a view of Mary Boleyn that was very different to that portrayed in most accounts. How had Mary managed to be the only one of Anne's ladies who wasn't interrogated about the accusations against Anne which led to her death? How had Mary managed to slip away quietly from the Court when she, George and Anne had been inseparable while George and Anne had left in their coffins? There was a big part of that story that had never been told. No, milksop Mary was no doubt a useful front but could not be true, Miranda needed to tread very carefully.

The sweet as honey smile was turned on Miranda, 'And how are you enjoying your time at Court Mistress Glover?'

'I am enjoying it very much Your Ladyship, Lady Marchant is most kind.'

'I am sure she is, and have you had the pleasure of being presented to the King?' There it was, the innocent question, the answer already known in the most minute of detail, setting the trap.

'Indeed, it was a great honour.'

Lady Marchant told Mary what she had come to find out, it would be known to all within hours anyway. 'The King has been kind enough to invite us to join him for the jousting, it is many months since I have enjoyed an entertainment such as this will be. Will we see you there Lady Mary?'

'If my sister is able to sleep a little I hope to be there, there is always so much to see at a joust, don't you think Lady Marchant?' The sweet face showed nothing but openness, the words were unimpeachable, but everyone in the room except Lady Maria heard the warning shots being fired. Lady Marchant could not help but think of the quiet dignity with which Queen Katherine would have handled such matters, never would anything have induced her to stoop to a display of jealousy or send anyone on an errand of common curiosity, how times were changed.

Later, as Betsy was brushing Miranda's hair until it shone in preparation for the afternoon, Miranda was struck with an idea and acted on it impulsively, 'Betsy, can you get me some paper and ink to write a letter please?' Within an hour, a letter from a well-wisher giving the coordinates of his missing ship and the details of the surrounding coastline and half hidden rocks was on its way to Lord Benedict, but by the time it reached him it had been read and copied by Boleyn spies. Betsy was loyal but the servant sent running with messages was easily bought.

An enormous shadow crept across Miranda's future, threatening to blot out her moment in the sun as surely as the mayfly is doomed to the briefest of existences.

◆◆◆

Chapter 14
The Jousting

Miranda was a picture to turn all heads as she walked through the heat of the day towards the jousting pavilions. The rather daring scarlet and cream of her gown was beautifully set off by the scarlet parasol edged with cream ribbon and the wide band of cream velvet worn as a choker at her neck.

She had been surprised when Lady Marchant had suggested the choker instead of her pearls, 'One must think ahead on jousting day. If you are asked for a favour, your handkerchief is pretty but the intimacy of removing the velvet band from your beautiful neck for the right man can be quite thrilling whilst remaining perfectly decorous.' Lady Maria had difficulty imagining her grandmother doing such things but recognized the voice of experience, she hurriedly changed her own handkerchief for the prettiest one she owned and sprinkled it with rosewater, just in case.

There was a definite stir as Lord Benedict escorted his grandmother, Maria and Miranda through the gathering crowds towards the King's pavilion. Lord Benedict did his best to be a chivalrous escort and companion but he was sorely distracted by the note that had reached him, could there really be news of his ship? Why had it come to him in such a way?

He did not dare ask for permission to leave Court on a festival day that meant so much to King Henry but on the morrow he would start the long journey to Sheerness coast accompanied by a small troupe of his most loyal men. Until then he had to live with this burning impatience and shaken equilibrium, he could speak of it to no-one until he knew if there was any truth in it, not even his grandmother as he could not bear to see her hopes risen only to be dashed. No-one knew better than she how much the fortune of the Marchants' hung by the slenderest wisp of hope now.

As they wove through the Lords and Ladies resplendent in their rich and colourful attire, there were many passing greetings and pleased smiles at seeing Lady Marchant again and many eyes used the bow or curtsey as an opportunity to take a long look at Miranda. The gentle stir changed to a distinct murmuring as the King left the pavilion to welcome the party as they approached. He was most solicitous that they should be made comfortable within the pavilion in a cool spot with an excellent view.

When Lady Maria and Lady Marchant were seated, King Henry asked Miranda if she would like to walk with him and see his horse who was being made ready for the joust. Miranda blushed with happiness and took his proffered arm as they strolled towards the jousting preparation area. She felt the heady power of knowing that every pair of eyes was watching and she thrilled as the crowd parted before them as each Courtier gave an elegant bow or curtsey as the King passed. He seemed so genuinely happy as he talked to her of his love of the joust and as mischievous as a young boy when he asked her if she had taken a small wager on him.

'Indeed your Majesty, I have never wagered, I am not sure I know how one does such a thing!'

'But would you wager on me if you did Mistress Miranda?'

His vivid, magnetic eyes held hers, it was as if there was no-one else in the world, the people around them and the noise faded into the background. Miranda felt such a pull in her body, it was a physical feeling, as if a bond of glowing golden light was forming between their hearts, one that could not be broken without dreadful pain.

'I would wager on you My Lord.' She looked at him with such frankness, no thought of games or artifice. Henry had spent his life surrounded by people who would say anything to gain some advancement from him, he felt the power of her honesty and heard the unspoken declaration of love, he covered her hand on his arm with his own, the touch of his skin sent a powerful feeling through the core of her very being.

The groom held the reins as the beautiful gleaming horse snorted and stepped proudly as the King and Miranda approached. The King was delighted with his steed and Miranda felt his excitement at the joust ahead, he was so high spirited.

'So Mistress Miranda, what if I was the stable lad and you were the dairy maid, would you still give me your pretty smiles?' He spoke quietly so that the words were almost whispered, making a secret world for just the two of them,

'Indeed my Lord, I think I might smile upon you! And what would you say if I was the dairy maid and you were the stable lad?' It was the naughtiest they had been together, the flirtation open and the desire acknowledged.

'I think I might sweep you up on a fast horse and gallop away with you to a place where stable lads and dairy maids look at the courting moon in the night sky together, with blood pulsing strong in the heat of the summer evening.' His face was filled with longing now, he was so close that she could feel his breath against her ear. 'And what would you give me in the light of the moon? What do you think would make me happy?' She reached up and touched his cheek so gently that he felt it in his very nerve endings, he gripped her upper arm, his control nearly lost.

They pulled apart reluctantly as The Duke of Suffolk was heard to approach looking for the King; in the final few moments that they were sheltered by the gleaming body of the horse Henry gently took the cream choker from her neck, his fingers lightly caressing the sensitive skin at the back of her neck as he did so. His eyes never left her face as he gently kissed the sweet-smelling fabric and tucked it slowly inside his tunic, every sensuous movement creating desire in her body, every fiber of her being longed for his touch, she longed to have him without another second's delay and to feel his hands on every part of her body, gently first and then urgently. Miranda felt almost shocked as they parted, the feelings were so intense, she was shaky as she returned to the pavilion and glad to sit down in the cool alongside Lady Marchant.

The King rode out in the most magnificent armour, the picture he made as he sat astride his superb mount would stay with Miranda forever, he was every inch the King, every inch the valiant knight, every inch the unvanquished hero of the hour. As he passed the royal pavilion he dipped his lance to Lady Marchant and her party, Miranda felt every eye upon her and she knew the feeling of being lifted up by the love of an all powerful man.

The jousts were more brutal than Miranda had thought, they were no show battles, as the King unseated two challengers one after the other she realised how dangerous it was and felt her desire for him grow even stronger as he showed his strength and courage. The thought of having that body on hers, so dominant as he soundly defeated those who were brave enough to stand against him, she felt almost faint with longing. She felt herself her body give way to its desire, she would have surrendered to him in the jousting field if he had commanded it. Miranda closed her eyes as her fantasy overcame her and she dissolved into her longing for the King. The fantasy blended with reality as she opened her eyes and saw him leaning over her, so close that only she could smell the musky male sweat that emanated from him after the triumphant performance at the jousting, he was the victor and he wanted the spoils. Only she heard the whispered words, 'Tonight, I must have you' her voice was husky with longing as she answered him with one word, 'Yes'.

Lady Marchant had been immensely put out that Miranda had not curtsied as the King approached but she could see by the looks on both their faces that she need not worry, there was no question of Miranda not being in favour.

◆◆◆

Chapter 15
The delicious gift

As soon as Lady Marchant realised that the King would send for Miranda that very night she swung into action as if for a military campaign.

Maria was immediately set to work to trim the neckline of the prettiest of Miranda's night shifts with soft ruffles of lace and tiny seed pearls. As she worked the rest of the shift was immersed in handfuls of dried rose petals and dried lavender, the sweet-smelling flowers being slightly crushed in the folds of the softest, dreamiest fabric with every change of position.

Maria was covered in petals as she worked, she looked like an ethereal creature from another realm, too pretty to be human. While she was in this guise of a maiden goddess, the handsome page from the musical evening arrived with a note for Lady Marchant; after all his maneuvering to be the one to bring the note he then wasted his opportunity by being so overcome that he could do nothing but stare and stammer and then curse himself once outside the door. If he could have seen the prettiest flushing of Maria's neck and cheeks as she carefully concentrated on her sewing he would have felt himself well rewarded and gone with a livelier step.

Betsy was organizing the bringing and filling of the bath, the wooden bath was lined with a fine linen sheet, no splinters would be allowed to mar the beauty of Miranda's soft and inviting skin tonight. Betsy scented the water with a heady blend of oils; honeysuckle, vanilla and almond formed a hazy sheen on the surface of the gently steaming water.

Betsy knew the blend of perfume her mistress would wear and selected her oils carefully to complement it, the oils would sooth and soften her creamy skin and sweetly fragranced hair too. Betsy laid out the comb and hairbrush, the evening was warm enough for Miranda's hair to dry at the open window, her beautiful honey gold tresses would be loose tonight, scented deliciously in every strand.

Even Lady Marchant was not as determined as Betsy that Miranda would be the most delectable gift for the King tonight, being part of the ritual of preparing the beautiful body for the King to take his pleasure of was a privileged honour. Giving the orders for the bath to be filled had set the servants' grapevine afire and Betsy was at the heart of it all, saying nothing with a satisfied expression that said everything. She was as demure and discreet as a novice nun when taking her orders from Miranda and Lady Marchant of course, never did she give the slightest hint that she knew what all the preparations were for.

Lord Benedict had been given his task, he was to stay close to the King to be on hand to come for Miranda when the King deemed the time to be right, apart from that he was banished from Lady Marchant's apartments. She was aware that Lord Benedict had feelings for Miranda, she wanted nothing to spoil the preparations, it was better for him not to be there but if escorting Miranda to the King's chambers would cause him pain then suffer he must. There was more at stake tonight than Benedict's feelings. Lady Marchant was well seasoned in the knowledge that feelings often passed with time but great gifts from Kings benefitted one's family for many generations to come and crossing Kings generally didn't end at all well.

Lady Marchant herself looked out a truly breathtaking hooded silk robe embroidered with gleaming silver threads and peacock blue pools of colour, it was a robe fit for a princess with slippers to match and Miranda would feel no shame in crossing the quiet parts of the palace to reach Henry wearing such an exquisite garment, only Henry would know that she wore just her delicate night shift beneath it, and nothing but the softness of her skin and the blended scents of her perfume beneath that.

Lady Marchant was nothing if not direct, after ensuring that she and Miranda were in totally private audience she said, 'Now my dear, I will instruct you on the night ahead, but first you must tell me if you are truly a maiden so I will know how to best advise you.'

Miranda's hesitated and Lady Marchant held up her hand to gainsay any speech, 'very well, you must not be frightened and I will be direct. Let the King know that you are a maiden when the opportunity comes, if he knows that he has taken your maidenhood he will be generous towards you when making provision for your future when the time comes for him to put you aside. You must be demure and let him lead you in all things, it will please him greatly and you can never be accused of wantonness if you have done only his bidding.' 'Lady Marchant, what if there should be a child from the King?'

'Then you will have assured your future and the future of your line Miranda, the King would look most kindly on you and your rewards would be many, may good fortune be with you tonight.'

Lady Marchant passed Miranda a tiny glass flask containing a viscous amber liquid, she loosened the glass stopper and the most luxurious and sensuous musky scents touched Miranda's senses in a place that she had never before been aware of, somewhere primal signaled it was awakening, there was a stirring, deep inside Miranda's body. 'What is it?' she gasped.

Lady Marchant smiled, 'The recipe is known only to the female line of my family and never before has anyone not of our blood been allowed to make use of it. Give it the king as a gift to ease any soreness from the jousting, tell him that you would be honoured to apply it if it could ease his achings. Even men as well served by beautiful women as the King will find themselves lost in feverish lovemaking when they feel these oils sliding over warm skins and breathe the scents that have driven men wild with lust over many centuries. It is as important a part of our heritage as our Lords prowess in battle, we never forget to what we owe it.'

Miranda knew that she would normally feel a little strange talking this way to someone as august and imposing as Lady Marchant but these were not normal times. She thanked Lady Marchant most sincerely for the precious gift and for the advice, she felt as if she was going into battle on behalf of the Marchants and had no intention of letting them down, she longed to conquer and to be conquered.

The next few hours passed in a sensuous dream as she was bathed, oiled, scented, dressed in the fine nightshift with the exquisite lace and pearl trimmings and finally wrapped in the silver and peacock blue robe, the most beautiful gift, ready to be deliciously and slowly unwrapped when it so pleased the King.

◆◆◆

Chapter 16

The conquering

Miranda was hardly aware of Lord Benedict at her side as she walked through the halls and passages of the palace when the summons came, her desire for Henry was blotting out all. The very small part of her thinking that still functioned had ensured that she had taken the key to the secret door from her neck and wrapped it with the fine chain in a silk handkerchief thrust deep in the pocket of the robe. It was the first time it had left her neck and even the thoughts of the night ahead could not drive from her mind the need to have the key with her at all times.

For Benedict's part, his mind was so conflicted with taking the treasured Miranda to Henry's bed and his desperate worry and dreadful hope for his ships that he could hardly think straight. He knew that he must wait outside Henry's chambers until Miranda was ready to be escorted back, he knew that the time would be the longest he had ever experienced whether it lasted an hour or until the morning light. He knew that he must smile and bow in the presence of the King and never show his true feelings for a second. He knew that the night would bring him pain for his own sake but that he was also impatient for it to be over so that he could begin his journey to Sheerness coast, it was a tangled confusion of thoughts, unbalancing even his clear-headed disposition.

They reached the doors of the chamber and the Kings men-at-arms lowered their weapons to allow Miranda and Lord Benedict to pass, Benedict bowed low but he could see that Henry had eyes for no-one but Miranda as he took her hand in his to raise her from her curtsey. Benedict murmured that he would take his leave with His Majesty's permission and as he left he saw Henry gently push back the hood of the beautiful robe, neither Henry nor Miranda were even aware that he had gone.

No words passed between them as Henry led her to a richly upholstered velvet couch. Then, with his own hands he poured her a goblet of the richest red wine, he filled his own goblet too and sat beside her, looking deeply into her eyes and raising the goblet gently to her lips. She felt the wine run sensuously over her tongue, the rich flavours of blackberries and vanilla setting her senses ablaze, the desire coming to the surface as she saw his lips part for the wine and wanted to dash the goblet from them and greedily cover them with her own, she knew she had to be demure but every part of her could feel the blood throbbing in her veins, her fingertips felt as if the blood must pulse through, she longed for his touch.

'I have a gift for you' she whispered the words, it was hard to speak. 'an oil for any bruises from the jousting, it must be applied with gentle hands.'

'Are your hands gentle Miranda?' He stroked the inside of her wrist, every cell in her skin came alive, her body yearned for him, it was a struggle to speak, her voice was hesitant.

'Yes my Lord, they are gentle.'

'Will you call me Henry? It would please me to hear my name on your lips,'

'Henry, may I soothe your sore muscles? It would give me such pleasure to do so.'

He slipped the robe from her shoulders and traced the neckline of her nightshift with his gentle touch, dipping in below the edge of the ruffled soft lace, just brushing the softness of her breast. He leaned forward, breathing in the scents of her hair and body, marveling at the softness of her skin, the honey silk of her hair.

'I would like that, my shoulders are a little sore, shall I kneel before you and you can ease the muscles?' Henry King of England knelt and removed his soft shirt, his skin glowing in the candlelight, his muscles defined and taut in his strong arms.

Miranda unstopped the phial and dripped a little of the oil onto his shoulder, then his other shoulder and his chest, the liquid dribbled down and she reached out and drew her fingers through the oil, feeling him shudder with longing beneath her touch as the scents of the oils reacted with his most primeval senses in a way he had not experienced since a young man come to lovemaking for the first time.

He wanted it to be slow, to take her as a maiden gently but he did not know if he could control it. She used both hands to smooth the oil onto his chest and shoulders, luxuriously gripping his arms as she slid her palms over his muscles. He urgently pulled loose the front of her nightshift and lowered his head to take her rosebud nipple in his mouth. Miranda grasped his hair gently, it was unbearable, Henry and the darkly musk scent of the oil was moving her mind and body to places it had never been, he pushed his body against hers and she felt the nightshift ride up, revealing the creamy softness of her skin. He took some of the oil on his own hand and stroked the inside of her thigh.

'Have you lain with a man before sweetling? his voice was broken, coming in short breaths as he tried to stay in control.

'No My Lord, I am honoured to give you my body, I want nothing more than to make you happy.'

'Will you do my bidding Miranda? Whatever I tell you to do?'

'Yes my Lord, I am yours in every way.'

Miranda longed for him but she must wait for his commands, she could not take the lead. He ripped off his remaining clothes and flung them to the floor, then silently he swept her up into his arms and carried her to the bed.

Hours later, when he had made both the sweetest and the most urgent love to her, slowly caressing every inch of her skin and marveling over the soft plumpness of her delicious curves, he held her close and whispered 'my sweetling, how has this come to be?'

Miranda replied with all honesty, 'I know not my Lord, I knew that some like it and some do not but never did I know that it would be like this.'

The King was serious and spoke with truth, 'It is not always like this, this is a place out of the daily world, where only lovers can visit and then only for the briefest of times, if we find it even once in our lives we have more than most ever will. You must go now, you cannot be here when the palace awakes.'

The King gently placed her robe around her shoulders and raised the hood with his own hands, he opened the door to his chamber and nodded briefly to Lord Benedict who struggled to present a Courtier's countenance as he quickly rose to his feet, Miranda passed silently into the ante room and the door closed behind her.

◆◆◆

Chapter 17
Palace spies

Lord Benedict escorted Miranda in silence through the passageways and halls, Lady Marchant was waiting with sweet warm rosewater ready in the washing basin, she left Miranda alone to bathe her tender body and put on a freshly laundered shift. The bed was already turned back, the cool sheets inviting, the lavender pillow would hardly be needed. Lady Marchant returned with spiced cake and a cool draught of elderflower cordial laced with healing herbs.

'He is pleased with you?'

Miranda nodded, her sleepy satisfied smile communicated all that Lady Marchant needed to know. She did not need to ask if the Marchant family recipe had created the desired outcome, she too had used its power to her own advantage and sometimes thought back to those times on dark nights when memory slipped free of daytime constraints.

There was no point in thinking that any young girl was going to keep her good sense around the King, there was need of a cooler and wiser head for that task. Lady Marchant knew that the King would be out hunting at dawn even though he too had been up half the night, she would make sure that Miranda did not try to match him. Miranda needed to renew herself with sleep, the bloom of beauty and vitality did not last forever and burning the candle at both ends would ensure it did not last at all, a lesson Anne Boleyn would have been wise to learn.

Miranda was a precious asset and would be lovingly cared for. It was little different to healing the wounds of the generations of Marchants who had done battle for their

King; loyal servants must be nursed back to their full power to serve the Crown in any way that was needed. Miranda was as much a returning warrior as any of them. Lady Marchant quietly closed the door as Miranda slipped into sleep, it was too early for Maria and Betsy to be stirring and they would be careful not to wake her.

Lord Benedict came to take leave of his grandmother, he told her that it was possible a nobleman in Kent had news of his ships, he had thought of many half-truths he could have told her but she would know he was hiding something. He told her to prepare for the worst news and did not tell her about the note from the well-wisher. A seasoned campaigner like his grandmother would have been instantly on the alert for intrigue, why would anyone do such a thing anonymously when they could have gained great favour from the Marchant family? He had the same thoughts but he was going to check the coast and seabed come hell or high water.

A handpicked advance party had already set out on the journey to secure the services and the discretion of the local expert divers. The Marchants ruled their lands with firmness and an even hand and in return demanded total loyalty of their soldiers, farmers and servants. Blackstone, Lord Benedict's man of business who commanded the advance party, would have laid down his life for the family and Benedict had entrusted him with the full story of the note.

However, Blackstone was not on the lookout for the Queen's spies who had ridden out before and behind them. The Boleyn spies were waiting at the rugged coast a full day before the advance party reached it, securely settled into a rocky cleft where they could see all without being seen.

'It may be two days' journey Grandmother so do not expect to see me back soon, I will write if there is urgent news to impart. The King has given me leave to see to my affairs.'

'Whether the news is good or bad we will weather it Benedict, we have resources other than wealth and we shall marshal them if needed.'

'Grandmother, let me give my best efforts to retrieving our fortunes before you embark on your ruthless winnowing of the heiresses of England.' Benedict kissed his grandmother's hand, even in this difficult time he had to smile, what a commander of an army she would have been! He had often felt that her manor, staff and grandchildren did not give enough scope to her talents, no wonder even the King called upon her for counsel.

The journey was dusty and hot, the men would have borne any hardship and scorned to show any flagging of their strength before their Lord but the horses must be rested properly and Benedict's frustration grew as the hours passed. He had faced the loss of his family fortune with fortitude, accepting that Maria's marriage chances would be much reduced if his ships were lost. He could not, would not, accept that his grandmother could lose her Manor house. Even if every other part of his estate went, his castle, the farms, the lands, he would save White Hart Manor for her.

He had no fears of his strength and courage and would seek commissions from the King to do what he could to restore his fortunes in time but it would be a hard blow to lose all his forefathers had fought and died for.

Blackstone was ready on the coast when they arrived, 'All is in place Lord Benedict, the descriptions of the coast and landmarks did not tally exactly with the co-ordinates, I have positioned the men to search using the written description first. The divers are waiting only for your signal, the boat is ready to take us out.'

Benedict was travel stained from the journey but he had no intention of waiting even another hour for the investigations to begin. He gave orders for the men and horses who were remaining on shore to be fed and watered and he and Blackstone rowed out to the larger diving vessel.

The diving began, with the men staying under water for longer than seemed humanly possible on each dive. Again and again they disappeared into the cold and gloomy depths, emerging to breathe and fan out slightly. As the light started to fail hope failed with it. Benedict's mood was black as he thought about potential enemies who could have sent that letter, he could no doubt count Anne Boleyn amongst them now that the Marchants were whoremasters for the King. How she would be laughing to think of him off on a wild goose chase to end in his dashed hopes and Lady Marchant's downfall. Anne would know they had no choice in the matter of standing friend to Miranda but that would not stop her blaming them; and no-one would be more sweetly disappointed for the loss of his fortune than milksop Mary Boleyn, whose angelic face sat strangely with her love of malice. If Benedict had known that the third sibling, George Boleyn, was at that moment positioned in a hidden cleft on the coast, spyglass firmly fixed on the diving vessel, his blood would have run cold.

A triumphant shout shattered the evening silence, one of the divers signaled to the others and all four dived again in the same spot. Within minutes the crew on the diving vessel were throwing over the marker buoys. The divers could identify enough of the ship for Benedict to know he had found The White Hart and he felt his heart thunder with the hope he had dared not set free until now. The ship had not broken up and there would be many of the drowned inside. Benedict made the immediate decision to let the men rest in their watery grave; retrieving their bodies would severely hamper the salvage operation and give nothing but distress and expense to the families. It could be seen as a harsh decision but it was his to make and he made it with no qualms, his role was to lead and command and he never shirked in his duty.

Blackstone sent for the salvage expert, all involved were being paid handsomely for their work and silence but things needed to move quickly. Lord Benedict sent a messenger to bring reinforcements to guard the wreck, if the dreamed of treasure was on board he would need them while the work went on. The last communication from the captain had included accounts of gold and uncut rubies of a size that would make even a King's heart beat a little faster if they were half true. Blackstone would not leave the vessel while the salvage took place, every item would be documented, every gold coin and every pearl accounted for. Benedict's ship had indeed come in and as the night fell fully he sent up a private prayer of thanks, hedged with caution until the contents were truly known.

By then a Boleyn spy was already beginning the journey back to London to report back to the Queen, the activity around the diving vessel had shown clearly that the directions had hit their mark. George Boleyn himself would remain until he saw evidence of actual treasure being retrieved; the note from the well-wisher was about to take centre stage at Greenwich Palace and its writer was blissfully unaware of the storm clouds gathering.

◆◆◆

Chapter 18

The calm before the storm

The gifts began to arrive in the early afternoon, first a most generous length of silk, shot through with iridescent greens against a forest green background, it was luxurious and surely unique in Britain, maybe one of the very finest silks from the Amsterdam traders. It was also the King's favourite colour as Lady Marchant well knew.

Then an invitation to a musical recital on the morrow, Miranda thought only about playing for the King again and was flustered to have enough time to practice and for Maria to help her, but Lady Marchant knew how very different this invitation was to the last one.   That had been an extremely private gathering, the King had been greatly discreet although he would never lower himself to secrecy. This was a recital to whom the King's closest courtiers would be invited, this meant that the first families of the realm would be forced to acknowledge Miranda as the King's welcome guest or risk offending him.

It had been easy for some of them to choose not to see her while they had dined in amongst the hundreds in the great hall, not so in this circumstance. There were many who would graciously overlook her lack of birth for Henry's favour or out of courtesy to Lady Marchant, however the hovering wrath of the Queen was a fearsome cloud over the Court and people walked carefully. It was even possible that the Queen would attend herself. That would be a situation to make all quake, with the marked exception of the King who had reached the final limits of appeasing the Queen's ill temper, was he King in his own Kingdom or not?

The piece de resistance arrived next; Maria was transfixed as Miranda opened the silver box lined with dove white velvet, Lady Marchant was hardly less fascinated and Betsy actually held her breath lest she be noticed and sent from the room. Miranda raised the exquisite necklace with both hands and the light struck the flawless precious stones. Hands quivering with excitement, Maria made fast the ornate gold clasp around Miranda's neck, the intricately worked gleaming links and the twelve perfect emeralds framed her beautiful throat and neck, only awed silence could do justice to the beauty of the moment.

'Betsy, attend to your work!' Lady Marchant's words sent Betsy scuttling from the room, but she thought the moment well worth the sharp rebuke.

'Miranda, my dear, if your time at Court should end tonight you will leave a wealthy woman.'

'The note says he will see me at the musical recital tomorrow so I hope I am not yet to leave, and … I would like to see him again, even if he sent me no emeralds.'

'Of course my dear, all lovers long for sweet words and kisses but giving you these wonderful gifts gives the King pleasure, you would not deny him that pleasure I think?'

'I could deny him nothing Lady Marchant, nothing at all.'

Lady Marchant glanced at Maria who was as moonstruck as Miranda with the romance of it all, these girls of marriageable age could rarely focus on the proper acquisition of wealth, lands and titles; family matriarchs had to be as vigilant in negotiations as any foreign Ambassador.

It was obvious that Miranda was not in the practical state of mind to summon the dressmakers to begin work on the silk gown. They would need to work all night so the sooner they began the better and Lady Marchant stirred up a hive of activity in no time at all.

The King had obviously pictured Miranda in the iridescent green silk set off with the emerald necklace and the King was not to be disappointed. Lady Marchant gave instructions for a gown that would cause ripples of envy in the ladies and waves of desire in the men. There was nothing immodest in the design, just a perfect setting for a ripe peach at the height of her beauty, the dipping of the bodice just enough to hint at the hidden pleasures beneath, the sleeves drawing attention to the delicate wrists and pretty hands. The skirt full enough to spread out gracefully as she took her place at the virginal, creating a tableau fit to enchant a King.

Miranda was set to work to practice at the virginal with Maria, the King would almost certainly ask her to play and she needed to be able to make a good impression amongst the exalted company. Miranda could hardly believe that she was to sing the heart wrenching beauty of the words and music of John Denver's 'Annie's song' for Henry VIII. Thomas Wyatt the Court poet might even be there to hear them too. In fact Miranda was having difficulty thinking about bringing the music and lyrics into Henry's time at all, the reality of her normal life was receding so fast, a time without Henry was not a time she wanted to live in.

Miranda did not practice late, she was sent early to bed with a draught of wine spiced with herbs to encourage sleep and soothe the nerves. First Betsy brushed her hair until it was smooth and glossy and then gently gathered it in a soft cotton cap with a little almond oil rubbed in for overnight beauty. A hot cloth of the finest lawn was dipped in the sweetest warmed rainwater infused with rose petals and her décolletage, shoulders, neck and face were gently cleansed and all traces of the day removed.

Under the supervision of Lady Marchant, Betsy dipped into the luxurious lotions that would be locked up again immediately afterwards and reverently applied the beautifying night oils to her Mistress's flawless skin. As the gleam of the oils lit the swell of her bosom and the curve of her shoulders glowed in the candlelight, Miranda wished she could go to the King tonight, the heady jasmine and honeysuckle scents made her long for Henry's hands to be upon her once more. Miranda was helped into the lavender scented bed and in this sensuous mix of perfumes and thoughts of desire she slept deeply.

As Miranda drifted off, Betsy rubbed the excess lotion from her hands onto her own face and neck, a very nice perquisite of being a lady's maid.

As Miranda slept, Anne Boleyn received her brother's messenger with Mary the only other witness to the tidings from Sheerness. She sent word to one of Henry's closest advisors to attend her the following evening when her brother returned.

As Miranda slept, Lord Benedict and Blackstone saw the first haul from the hold of the ship, this time Lord Benedict's prayers of thanks were not constrained.

As Miranda slept, George Boleyn put down his spyglass and mounted his horse. As Miranda slept, the Boleyn spies gave Mary the news of the Emerald necklace, no-one dared to give the news directly to Anne.

◆◆◆

Chapter 19
The storm breaks

As Lady Marchant entered the recital room with Maria and Miranda she could be forgiven the sin of pride on this occasion. Maria had a bloom about her that nothing other than youth and the lightest whisper of first love could bring, her gown was of the palest lilac and trimmed with the prettiest lace and seed pearls suitable for the youngest of girls at Court. Her bearing was modest and her curtsey demure; although she kept her eyes downcast she knew exactly where the handsome page was in the room, she saw him at the edge of her vision and felt his attention on her as if it was a physical energy between them. Her nervousness was mirrored by his, but neither of them could resist furtive glances at the other.

Every head in the room turned as Miranda made her curtsey to the King. The glorious colours of the gown had never before been seen at Court, blending and weaving together as Miranda lowered her graceful head and neck in obeisance to the King and all watched as he took her hand to raise her. The necklace was dazzling, every head reckoned its cost and made a mental note to find out where it had come from. The word was that Miranda was of very humble birth but this display of richness seemed to contradict that. If it was a gift from the King, then this was no fleeting dalliance to be put casually aside when the Kings interest was caught elsewhere.

Henry was most solicitous in ensuring that Lady Marchant and Maria sat near him, with Miranda in the beautiful seat alongside his own, the upholstery embroidered with snowdrops and freesias. If anyone present was put out by the attention given to the Marchant party, they were very careful not to show it. It was a gathering of people who had lived their whole lives as beautifully mannered courtiers, charm and grace were their stock in trade and as long as Henry favoured them the rewards were very ample indeed. They had smiled at Katherine, then at Anne and would gladly now smile at Miranda. Every single person was wondering what would happen if Anne arrived; husbands and wives and mothers and daughters had to display the firmest self discipline to hold back their speculations until they were in the safety of their own chambers, and even then, you could never be sure.

The Court musicians played the first songs, bringing some of Henry's own compositions to life, the beauty of the music touched Miranda's soul and she could not but shed some tears as the notes and melodies evoked the deepest and sweetest of emotions. Henry was well pleased and leaned over to cover her hand with his as she touched her delicate handkerchief to her tears at a particularly beautiful piece. They looked at each other and Miranda saw the musician, the composer, one whose music was precious to him and he sent it into the world with the same hesitations and vulnerability as any other artist, afraid lest the world should not receive it kindly and no royal crown could protect him from that. She felt so grateful that the music was of a rare beauty, to think that she was hearing this in Henry VIII's own Court, at a time when it was new and Henry was at the peak of his musically creative powers. Again she felt the most unbearable tug of emotional pain in her body and heart as she thought of the sorrow to come for Henry when his physical powers would be so tragically altered with the dreadful injury to his leg, surely there was some way she could avert this?

This time it was Henry's turn to recognise Miranda's apprehension as she rose to take her place at the virginal with Maria to turn the music. The private smile he gave her said so much, for just a moment he was not the richly attired and all powerful King, for just a moment he was a man in love, there only to let his lady know that she need not be nervous, that he believed in her.

The beautiful music of Annie's Song filled the room as Miranda's hands moved with grace and beauty over the keys of the virginal. It felt as if her heart was in her words as she sang the opening line for him as if no-one else was in the room. The company was dumbstruck, as 'You fill up my senses like a night in the forest' began a musical awakening that no-one would ever forget. The courtiers knew that this was something very different, that their King's new companion was no empty beauty to be disregarded outside of the bedchamber.

But the biggest impact was on the musicians, they were incredulous, they could hardly believe the evidence of their own ears, where had this come from? Had this lady really composed such a piece? They must have the music, they must have the lyrics, they must hear it again. The silence was absolute when Miranda finished playing, people felt as if they were recovering from an emotional thunderstorm, finding it hard to regain their equilibrium. Then the applause began, it was not polite, it was thunderous, even the most seasoned of the courtiers did not think about the impression they were making, this was the most genuine display of feeling that room had seen for many years. Henry could see that one of his chief musicians was wiping away a tear and beckoned him forward.

'Well? What do you think of my musical find?'

'Your Majesty, I am without words, I feel the emotions but cannot express them properly. May I have your permission to ask the Lady if she will allow us to see the music and lyrics?'

'You shall ask her yourself Webber' and Henry raised Miranda from the seat at the virginal and Webber made his bow to her, he bowed low in genuine appreciation of her musical ability, even the fact that she had the favour of the King was forgotten.

When Miranda understood what was being asked of her she turned shyly to the King, 'Your Majesty, if you would do me the great honour of accepting this song as a gift from your humble subject then it would give me much pleasure if you were to decide its fate from this moment on.'

Henry was much pleased, 'We are happy to accept your gift Mistress Miranda' he swept an elegant bow and instructed Webber to have copies made of the music and return the original to him. 'I shall treasure it Mistress Miranda', there was a truth in those simple words that vibrated along the bond of golden light that seemed to have been woven between their hearts.

Webber had to relieve the handsome young page of the music that he was carrying for Maria as if she could not be expected to bear such a burden, he was the only person in the room who had been almost oblivious to the beauty of the music, he had eyes and ears only for the sweetest girl who ever turned a page.

The party was served spiced wine and sweetmeats and many made their way to Miranda to pay their compliments, she received them modestly and in no time the story of the humble scholarly father who loved music and learning had reached the ears of all present. The necklace was not a family heirloom then and at least there was no maneuvering family hungry for places in all the King's affairs.

King Henry asked Miranda if she would give him the pleasure of a walk in the summer evening's air on the lawn that was reached directly from the reception room, others of the company strolled outside too, enjoying the feeling of being given licence to do so by the happy example of their King. Taking his arm felt delicious, she marveled that this wonderful man was the same one who had given her such delights in the bedchamber, she blushed now to think of it. His heart was too full to speak much of the song, he was too deeply touched by it.

'If only all my hours could be spent so sweetly Mistress Miranda, this evening has been balm for my soul.'

'It makes me so happy to give you pleasure Your Majesty and if I can dare to think that my small efforts help you in any way then I cannot imagine greater happiness.'

'Whisper my name sweetling, I would be your stable lad again this night if you will come to me.' Henry looked at her with such love that she could hardly help catching her breath.

'Henry' she whispered, 'I will come to you, I have thought of nothing else since we parted.'

'Henry!' louder, but no-one was close enough to hear. 'I have not thanked you for my wondrous gifts, I can scarce believe that I am wearing such a gown and necklace!' Henry loved to be the giver of gifts and he could see the genuine amazed appreciation,

'The emeralds cannot match your beauty but they must do their poor best. Now I must do my duty by my other guests or they will be affronted and I will have Dukes and Earls with sour faces.'

Miranda laughed, 'well I will promise you only sweet words and kisses when we meet again, and I will be more fortunate than any Duchess for I will have you all to myself.'

Anne observed the scene in the garden with mounting fury, she was positioned at a window but could not keep still in one place, the fury coursed through her veins and drove her to pace back and forth, bitterly seeing her loss and the nobody's rise.

After all she had done for the ungrateful King; she had worked tirelessly for his emancipation from the barren Queen and the rule of the Pope; she had entertained him ceaselessly; been the vibrating heart of every masque, dance and jousting fayre; enchanted all and sat tirelessly at her books to be able to converse with the King in all things; she had given him the Princess Elizabeth and tried with her very life to give him a son; she had danced late and ridden out with him early, fearlessly taking every ditch and fence to be his match in all things; and she had given him her body and sated his in more ways than most people could imagine, to keep a man on the edge without giving all for so many years was wearying beyond measure.

She felt so old, old before her time with the sheer exhaustion of being all things to Henry and to the Court. The fury she felt now gave her some of her old spirit but the collapse afterwards would be so hard. Now, every time she had to shine for the King or the Court the terrible draining away of all energy would take place as soon as she was alone and it was harder and harder to wear the mask.

She did not know if she could keep doing it, having the King dancing to her tune had fed the spiraling frenzy of activity but her power over him had all but passed, she knew it even if she could not bear to know it. Mary's scorning words about the nobody had been wrong, Kings do not hand out emerald necklaces to passing fancies, Anne thought she could see a gleam at the nobody's neck when the King and Miranda passed under a lit torch and her fingernails dug so hard into her palms that they drew blood.

Anne nursed the knowledge of the note with a bitter calm beneath the frantic pacing. As soon as George should come, Henry's advisor would surely take the copy of the shipwreck letter with its provenance to the King. Anne would be very sure that words of witchcraft were whispered, there may be other ways the nobody had known where the ship was but even the suspicion of witchcraft would be enough.

With every fibre of her being she mentally entreated George to come soon, in two more hours she would wager the King would have the nobody in his bed and even his closest advisors would not dare disturb him then. Anne felt the rage build at the thought and then she collapsed onto the window seat as the rage ebbed away into the terrible exhaustion that left her empty, shaking, defeated.

Miranda returned to Lady Marchant's apartments to find the scented bath already filled, she removed the beautiful silk gown and stepped into the gently steaming water. Maria was allowed to attend her and laughed as she saw Miranda with the emeralds still about her throat as she luxuriated in her second bath of the day, an unheard of extravagance.

'Indeed Miranda, should all ladies wear jewels for bathing now?'

'Well Maria, one would hope that you will never enter the water without at least a ruby or two!' The girls giggled together, neither girl had a sister and Maria could not remember her mother, to have a friend to share a moment of high spirits warmed both their hearts.

Maria told how the handsome young page had secretly passed her a small bloom, a shyly given flower of heart's ease and asked if she ever walked in the far gardens in the mornings.

'What time do you think counts as morning Miranda? I shall be too excited to sleep late but would it be unseemly to be there too early?'

'I shall walk with you as you must have a chaperone. We shall walk out at mid-morning, giving him time to start losing hope but not to despair. If nothing else we must find out his name!'

Maria was delighted, she helped Miranda scent her hair and body with almond, honeysuckle and vanilla oils and perfumes and put on the sweetly scented freshly laundered night shift trimmed with the pearls and lace. They knew not when Henry would send for Miranda and it was better to be ready early than to risk keeping the King waiting.

Miranda removed the emeralds and put the chain with the key in a silk handkerchief in the deep pocket of the peacock blue and silver robe; as lost as she was in this life a tiny cautious part of her mind could never forget to carry the link to her own world.

They sat peacefully with Lady Marchant in the candlelit room as the night drew on, at last the expected knock came. With a wildly beating heart Miranda rose as the servant opened the door. There are times when breeding and character really count and Lady Marchant's aristocratic background was in evidence as she greeted Lord Cromwell with every appearance of pleasantly surprised cordiality, not even an indrawn breath showed that she knew that this was bad news, very bad news indeed.

◆◆◆

Chapter 20
The undoing

Cromwell bowed to the ladies and all three returned deep curtseys. Maria was still under the impression that this was Miranda's escort come to take her to the King but Miranda recognized Cromwell immediately, she had seen his famous portrait many times. Not even Hans Holbein could do justice to the keen intelligence that marked him as no ordinary man, his remarks were mild but the sharp sweep of his intense eyes missed nothing.

Lord Cromwell entered the room quite alone, his escort took their places outside the door to ensure no interruptions.

'Leave us' Lord Cromwell's instruction to Betsy and the other servant in attendance was rapidly complied with. The guards at the door ushered them into an adjacent room, there would be no opportunities for any communication to anyone or for any letters or other evidence to be removed without Lord Cromwell being aware of it.

'Lady Marchant, I would like to ask Mistress Miranda some questions, would you be kind enough to allow me to do that here? I can of course arrange for somewhere else if this would inconvenience you.' Lady Marchant knew well where somewhere else was likely to be, something was very wrong but Lord Cromwell's courtesy and willingness to conduct talks here instead of at the Tower may mean that all was not yet lost.

'Of course Lord Cromwell, would you like me to stay?'

'I think not, if you and your granddaughter would be kind enough to retire to your bedchambers that would be very helpful, having you close at hand would mean that I can call upon you if needed.' Lady Marchant knew full well that it meant that she could not get a message to Lord Benedict or anyone else who may be able to help them.

'Come Maria. Miranda, give Lord Cromwell all possible help if you know anything that can assist him.' She swept from the room, followed by a still bewildered Maria. If truth be told Lady Marchant was baffled by the particulars too, of the general concern she had no doubt, someone was out to bring down the King's new favourite.

Cromwell was nothing but mild and gentle, his voice was never raised, his courtesy never faltered. He asked her of her father the scholar, he asked her of her home in Cumberland, he asked her of her learning and languages, he asked her how she came first to Court, he asked her of her poetry and music. Every answer brought forth another question, he had been to Cumberland, she must tell him of the exact location of her home, he would know it.

His voiced admiration for her poetry and music was followed with close questioning on the vellum and ink used on the books, he had traded and travelled across many lands and seen nothing like them, there was no detail too small to interest him and there was nothing she could say that would satisfy him. She did not even try to tell him that she had accidentally joined the masked ball, she immediately confessed that a servant had helped her to meet the King and that she would not reveal the name. He gave a dry smile at the thought that this girl thought she would decide what would and would not be revealed if he chose to pursue the matter, 'It may not be important, if it is we will return to the question.'

Cromwell could see that her story was full of holes, it may be that she was a lowly born girl who had used her assets of quiet beauty and a fine mind to play for the biggest prize in the land. He even had a respect for such boldness, it was not too different to his own approach although he had used his colourful background to enhance his reputation as a man to be reckoned with, not an option available to a woman.

He was intrigued by the calibre of her mind, she obviously was learned in languages and music and poetry, Cromwell found it credible that she had written the poem and the song lyrics and music, she openly confessed that she had another poem ready to give to the King and gave it to him. He read 'If you painted your life' silently, paying respect to her gifts as a wordsmith with a nod and just the word, 'indeed'. Her style was very different to anything he had come across in his wide travels and reading, evidence of a truly original mind. She seemed on solid ground when talking of the small portfolio of work he had seen, very different to the shaky discussion on where she had lived with her father.

Miranda felt as if she could risk breathing again, in the pocket of the blue and silver robe she grasped the key to the secret door so hard that she thought it must leave an imprint on her palm.

At last he came to it and of all the things it could have been she had not thought of this. Silently he handed her the copy of the letter she had sent to Lord Benedict, her hand shook almost imperceptibly as she took it from him, but he saw it.

'I know nothing of this Lord Cromwell, I do not understand.' Cromwell looked at her steadily, he knew had her measure.

'Indeed, then the writer must be Lady Marchant or Lady Maria as it certainly came from these chambers. I am sorry to have troubled you. Would you be kind enough to ask the Lady Maria to attend me in your place?'

Miranda's physical agitation told Cromwell all, 'Mistress Miranda, let us not waste each other's time further. I know you sent the message, I also know that the information you provided has resulted in The White Hart being found and its treasures are being raised as we speak. What I do not know is how you knew such a thing.' Cromwell was not a man who was afraid of silence, he steepled his fingers and looked at her with a mildly enquiring expression, with seemingly infinite patience.

Miranda felt the panic that had begun to subside peak sharply and overwhelm her thinking brain. 'I wish to see the King, he is expecting me.' Instinctively she reached out for her protector.

'He is aware of our discussion Mistress Miranda, he will understand if you are unable to join him.' Cromwell's impassive expression did not alter.

'I overheard some men discussing it when I was travelling, I knew I should not have been listening so I was afraid to give the information openly, they seemed like rogues and ruffians.' Perspiration stood out on Miranda's forehead.

'Very commendable' Cromwell's dry tone left her in no doubt of his scepticism. 'So, let us think on this a little, we have a young lady who as we both know is uncommonly intelligent and extremely resourceful. On finding that she has knowledge that could benefit a wealthy family she travels many miles and gains access to Greenwich Palace by subterfuge to pass on the information. One may wonder why such a resourceful person did not simply send a note from the nearest Inn? One may also wonder how she found out that The White Hart was connected to the Marchant family and why such blackguards and ruffians were so oddly indiscreet as to discuss their plans within earshot of a stranger?'

Miranda was cornered, she could see no way out, what could she say that could possibly pass muster?

Cromwell breathed a small sigh as if he wished such a task did not fall to him. 'Mistress Miranda, it is better if you tell me whether you have used any methods of divination, the penalty for witchcraft must be severe as you know but it may save you some distress if you are truthful.'

Miranda felt as if she would never be able to catch her breath, to be accused of witchcraft at Henry's Court was to be sentenced to death, and an interrogation that might have one begging for the mercy of the executioner's axe sooner rather than later.

'My Lord, ...' Miranda was stumbling for the words, she could not defend herself, 'It is not true, I am no witch My Lord.'

'Then explain your knowledge of the sunken ship if you please?' Miranda bowed her head, her hand clutched the key desperately, she had to get back to her own time, this wasn't going to end well. 'It came to me in a dream My Lord, I know not how.'

'Indeed, and what did you do prior to sleeping to bring on such a dream?' Cromwell, lawyer, interrogator of Cardinals and Dukes, need do nothing other than mildly voice the workings of a mind that had led many to a tangle of such despairing confusion that there was no way back.

'Nothing, nothing!' the words burst from Miranda, his very calmness was far more terrifying than any menace or threats could have been.

Cromwell rose and offered Miranda his hand 'Mistress Miranda, I believe that a night's undisturbed rest will help you remember, I will escort you to a peaceful room where you can think without interruption. Your maid can send on what you need.'

Miranda took his hand and stood up it was impossible to hide the trembling, 'Lady Marchant?' she whispered.

He did not answer, he gestured for her to walk alongside him and they set off, heading for the Great Hall. As they passed through the edges of the Hall, Miranda saw the King surrounded by courtiers, Lady Jane Seymour was gazing adoringly him as he talked. Miranda's whole body flooded with relief,

'Your Majesty!'

as the words escaped her lips, their eyes met for the briefest of seconds before he sharply twisted his body so that he had his back to Miranda and every part of his attention was focused on Jane Seymour. In that split second of ice cold rejection it was as if a physical pain winded her, she felt her knees weaken and she stumbled; Cromwell immediately supported her as he continued their progression without ever missing a step, uttering a word or slowing the pace. Even the terror of the position she was in could not blot out the terrible pain of the heartbreak.

She sank onto the floor of the room she was taken to and the door was locked behind her. She felt a physical tearing of the golden band of light that had flowed from her heart to his, the pain was indescribable. There was no hope, she had not been mistaken, his love was stone cold and gone from her. She could not switch off her longing in the same way, the harsh sob that escaped her throat was strange and frightening, nothing like it had ever emerged from her throat before, it was a primeval howl of pain and despair. She had been walking in joy and the terrible reality of the harshest of rejections could only find release in the most primitive way, she drew her body into a tight ball, as if to protect her poor battered being from the pain, but it could not be done. It was a heart rending dry sobbing and only one solitary tear emerged during those terrible hours of acute heartbreak, the pain was beyond tears. It tore at her and in her mind's eye she repeatedly saw the one person who could have given her solace sharply avert his face.

◆◆◆

Chapter 21
The longest day

Now came the longest day of Miranda's life, as the early pale pink of dawn touched the edges of the night, she rose painfully from the floor of the chamber and fell exhausted onto the bed, every joint of her poor body seemed to ache and her movements were slow and shaky, she felt so old, so profoundly weary.

A patch of sunlight moved a few inches across the walls and floor as each hour crept by. The shadow bars wavered, grew more solid as the sun reached its mid-afternoon intensity and then wavered again as time made its slow progress towards the evening.

An unknown maid appeared with a clean gown and shift, there was no note but sprigs of lavender fell from the folds and Miranda knew Betsy's care in that small gesture. The maid freshened the water jug, replaced the chamber pot and brought ale, bread and meats. She never spoke and the door stood open at all times she was in the chamber, the two guards at the door silently closed and locked the door as the maid left the room.

Miranda hurriedly washed and dressed, not to be caught unawares when Cromwell should return, then sat carefully in the upright chair for the same reason; but as the day crept on the dreadful tension of being on edge waiting for him every minute could not be sustained and she lay down on the bed, watching the shadows on the wall. At times she could just hear passing sounds from the Palace or grounds but faintly, the walls were thick and the window overlooked no public areas.

Miranda could not hope for the King to relent and send for her, she knew it would not be. Her heart though would not bear the logic of her knowledge and she could not help returning to the thoughts of when they had talked and danced and he had picked the sweetest bloom just for her, could he really have turned against her so quickly? Did she really mean nothing to him now?

The more frightening thoughts were of Lady Marchant and Maria, if Miranda was suspected of witchcraft they would be questioned, were perhaps being questioned at this very minute and perhaps Betsy too. It was unbearable to think that she had brought this upon them, and the consequences unthinkable if she, and perhaps they, were found to have any taint of witchcraft upon them.

Even then, it did not occur to Miranda to blame the King for any of this, the rawness of his betrayal had not yet turned to anger. If only a fury could have erupted from her very heart and soul at the man who had turned the Marchant family's lives upside down so he could have whatever whim took his fancy. If only a cold reckoning could have appraised how little he cared for putting them in a position where they must make bitter enemies who could lash out at them but not at the one who deserved it. If only she could have had bitter thoughts of how long it would take the King to order that the emeralds were returned to him. These thoughts could not sit with the love she still felt for him, instead she blamed herself for bringing misfortune to the Marchants, not yet able to come to terms with what scant regard the King looked upon friendship and loyalty and yes, even love. What he wanted, he took, and when he didn't want it any more no-one dared call him to account for his lack of honour that marked the man for what he was.

She wondered how long Cromwell would leave her in silence and solitude, she had no doubt that this was deliberate, how many days of this would it take to confess to anything that was put to her? Miranda made a deliberate decision to eat and sleep, her only hope was to be able to somehow reach the secret door in the alcove. How that chance would come she did not yet know, but at some point she would surely be moved elsewhere, if she was taken out of Greenwich Palace she would never get back to London in her own time and all would be lost.

She had to try and recover her mental and physical balance, slowly she ate the bread and meats and drank the ale, then she lay down and did what she could to calm her thoughts; eventually the exhaustion of not having slept for so long overcame her and she slept deeply. The gown that had been sent for her was not really suitable for sleeping in but she would not make herself vulnerable by sleeping in her shift, she kept her shoes on too. The key to the secret door was wrapped in her handkerchief and tucked deep inside her gown, the madness of being at the bidding of the King was ebbing and her researcher's mind was telling her to eat, sleep and prepare.

The slightest suspicion of the dawn was lighting the edge of the night's sky when she heard the whisper, it seemed to be inside her ear, so close that she felt the breath as part of the whisper.

'Say nothing, stay quiet, I am here to help you.' He repeated it three times, until he saw her nod in the dimness of the room and then he whispered, 'It's me, Benedict' and gently removed his hand from her mouth. He put his finger to her lips and he whispered again, 'I have but one chance to save you, follow me and say not one single word or we both die this night.'

Miranda rose silently, she followed him through the open door and past the lifeless bodies of the guards. They moved noiselessly through narrow passages in the silence of the sleeping Palace, Miranda felt that they were skirting the Great Hall but she could not be sure, she had to put all trust in Lord Benedict, silently she positioned the handkerchief holding the key to the secret door at the bosom of her gown. Benedict had chosen his hour well, he moved onwards, making for the side door that would enable him to reach a hidden path to the river unseen.

At the very moment his hand reached out to draw back the first heavy bolt, a guard stepped silently from the shadows and violently thrust the point of a small dagger into the base of the side of his neck, the point broke the skin and blood trickled down into his jerkin, 'Stand' hissed the guard. With lightning speed Lord Benedict threw himself backwards and brought down the guard by kicking his feet from under him as part of the same action. His shout of 'run!' was matched by the guard's shout of 'Guards!' and noise suddenly erupted, running feet and clanging swords could be heard as guards tried to find the source of the noise.

Miranda ran, she ran for her life, her shoes slapping against the stone flags as she dashed down a pitch black passage, her heart thundering in terror, her breath coming in rasping gasps as she asked more of her body than she had ever believed it could give. The terror drove her on and the tiniest sliver of grey light marked a doorway, she was beyond thought now and she burst through it, into the Great Hall from one of the servants' entrances. The shouts of 'Halt!' did not even enter her consciousness, she ran towards the secret alcove, moving so fast that the startled guards had no chance of cutting off her escape route, they were close behind though and she had literally seconds to get the key in the lock. Her mind and body reached the very limits of the reserves they had been calling upon and she collapsed on the floor of the alcove, completely physically and mentally spent.

Some time later she found herself cold and stiff on the floor in the silence of the Old Naval college at Greenwich, raising herself slowly, she steeled her jangled nerves. Once more she put the key in the lock and stepped through, once more the sounds of the masked ball greeted her, once more she turned the key again and stepped back to her own time to reset all that had happened. As surely as he had saved her she saved Lord Benedict from the moment where the guards had him cornered, at last she could go home.

◆◆◆

Chapter 22
The aftermath

Finding her things and getting changed and then making her way home seemed like herculean task. She slipped quietly out of the silent building as the caretaking staff opened up for the day. She had to get a taxi, she could not have made her way across London by tube in the state she was in, she wasn't even sure what day it was and if she should be back home yet.

The kettle was the catalyst, the very normality of the click of the switch as the water came to the boil started the trembling. By the time Miranda had made herself a cup of boiling hot tea and was sitting at her kitchen table with her fingers wrapped around the comfort of the mug in the still early morning light, she was shaking. By the time she had eaten four digestive biscuits she was light headed and only just able to make it to bed, she couldn't even shower. The note from Alice said she was away at a conference and Miranda had only enough coherent thought to be grateful that she didn't need to explain.

Sleep was almost instant and the turmoil and danger crashed across her dreams, making no sense as the King became a serpent and Maria dissolved into a cloud-like substance every time Miranda tried to stop her from falling from a window. When thirst woke her, Miranda stumbled to the kitchen, gulped down two glasses of water and made her way back to bed to sleep for a further six hours, when she woke again she was calmer, letting her thoughts arrange themselves in the safety of her own room. As evening came, she sank gratefully into a deep comforting bath and then wrapped herself in her bathrobe and lay down on the sofa.

Toast with melted cheese and a mug of tomato soup added to the feeling of being home, she was overwhelmed with appreciation for her flat and for Alice.

The peace allowed her to think clearly, perhaps for the first time since the madness with King Henry had begun. One thought stood out above all others, Lord Benedict had risked all for her; his life, his family, his fortune; she was so thankful for the last drop of energy that had ensured his safety when she had reset time. He was without his fortune now as no note had ever reached him but at least he was alive and Lady Marchant and Maria would still be living quietly at White Hart Manor. Never had Miranda seen with such clarity how much risk there had been for the family in doing the King's bidding.

Miranda knew she still had the power to change the fortunes of the Marchant family with her knowledge of the shipwreck. Now that she knew how one false step at Court could be the undoing of anyone with an enemy there, she would never act so recklessly again; she would help Lord Benedict but she must not put herself or any of the family at risk. There was no immediate urgency, time would be in the same place when she had thought it through with a clear head.

Above all she must spend a few days recovering and thinking, thinking it through right to the end of each possible path, not rushing in where even the most naïve angel would surely fear to tread. Another round of cheese on toast while flicking through the TV channels for the first time in weeks gave Miranda a profound feeling of contentment, almost as if she was a very little girl again with her Mum and Dad had both still alive, 'stuff the emeralds' she murmured out loud and even the pang she felt for her mother's pearls, lost forever in time, could not spoil the moment.

The next morning's sun rose on a Miranda who felt as if she had the beginnings of a plan. She spent some hours writing out different versions of a letter to Lord Benedict, then testing it from every angle to see if he could be accused of witchcraft or treason or anything else for receiving such a message. She sat at her kitchen table, with the sun lighting up the room and the radio playing quietly in the background. She heard the neighbours upstairs heading off to work and felt a rush of love for them that would have startled them very much if they had known; who knew whether positive thoughts really had an impact, if they did then the neighbours were in for a great day.

Miranda felt quietly satisfied with the final version, she read it over one last time.

In the year of Our Lord 1535

Lord Benedict

I have news of The White Hart, it has been shipwrecked off the coast of Sheerness, it lies approximately one mile out to sea at ship's coordinates 51°28'04"N 00°47'12"E

Many years ago your father saved mine from dishonour. I now hold the family debt repaid and my duty to my father's memory done.

I remain your humble servant.

Miranda spent a focused hour copying the letter onto vellum, working carefully with ink and a calligraphy pen to make it as authentic as possible. She knew enough from her academic research to spell and form the letters correctly but she checked every single point in her reference books, she was working to keep the Marchants' safe, it was a sacred responsibility. When she was sure that the ink was completely dry, she folded the paper and sealed it with warmed manuscript sealing wax. The calligraphy set contained an actual seal as well as the red wax sticks but she did not dare to use it in case it was the actual seal of any individual in Lord Benedict's time, she wanted no-one's life on her conscience.

Miranda walked to the local deli to pick up some lunch, she strolled back carrying her goats cheese, tomato and basil salad and felt a rush of happiness, her flowery skirt ruffled around her knees in the warm breeze and her white cotton top let the sunshine get to her bare arms. It was the most peculiar feeling to know that she had something very important to do that almost literally had no deadline. As long as she went back to save Lord Benedict at any point before she died then he would get the help at the exact same point in time. A supremely practical voice started listing all the things that could go wrong with this train of thought and she had to tell her own personal Jiminy Cricket to calm down, she was on it!

Miranda felt as if she was mentally firing on all cylinders again, she wondered if she had been temporarily unbalanced while she had been so obsessed with Henry, she actually laughed out loud as she imagined explaining her recent experiences to someone and telling them that the only thing that made her wonder if she was unbalanced was how much she wanted the King!

After her lunch and a glass of cloudy lemonade with some fresh mint, Miranda found out everything she could about the Marchant family on line and printed it off. It was very little, they had existed and built White Hart Manor, the family was basically a footnote in the history of the house. Miranda felt sad as she thought about what Lady Marchant would have said if she could read this, then she realised that Lady Marchant would have spent zero time on self pity and would probably have been too busy running some sort of super successful business to worry about whether she had lost out in the past. Miranda smiled, who knew that your role model was going to have lived 500 years before you?

Miranda gathered together her plain day gown, shoes and the letter to Lord Benedict and set off for the Old Naval College on the site of Greenwich Palace. As always, the key was on the chain around her neck and her hair was twisted into the prettiest of loose knots, as becoming now as in Tudor England. The tube wasn't too bad at this time of day even in the warmth of the summer and Miranda took pleasure in walking the last mile or so. There were crowds of tourists walking around the immaculate grounds and people had the most wonderful views of the college as they took trips on the river boats.

Miranda walked to the very spot where Henry had picked the beautiful budding rose for her, it was part of a different garden now, no longer a hidden place where lovers could whisper to each other but the sweetness of the moment would stay with her forever. She slipped inside, enjoying the cool of the interior, edging past the groups of people who were listening intently to the guides talking about the history of the building in its current and previous incarnations.

It was the work of moments to disappear into the shadows of the alcove and quickly change into her gown. Miranda knew that this would likely be the very last time she would go through the secret door and as she turned the key she prepared herself for the unnerving sensations. She felt apprehension too, what if the point in time had changed and she ended up back with the palace Guards? As the unsteady feeling passed she could hear the music of the masked ball playing again and felt her body flood with relief, keeping to the edge of the Great Hall, away from where she knew the King would be dancing she beckoned a servant to her. He was a little unsure of how to react, she was no grand lady in a bejeweled gown and mask but no lady's maid either. Miranda realised how quickly she had become accustomed to having servants and her tone and expression brooked no nonsense as she gave him her orders to deliver the message to Lord Benedict Marchant, leaving no doubt as to her status.

As the boy made his way around the Great Hall towards Lord Benedict, the King swept into view amongst the dancers, leading Lady Jane Seymour in her pale blue gown. Even Lady Jane's ornate silver and sapphire eye mask could not hide the open adoration in her face as she looked at Henry. Miranda's heart gave a terrible tug of pain and she felt the band of golden light wrench itself from her being, even at this dreadful moment she recognized the beginning of the end of the madness.

Across the Hall, Miranda saw Lord Benedict call the boy back sharply as he read the note, the boy looked round and pointed towards her and she started to walk quickly towards the hidden alcove as Lord Benedict set off towards her. As she reached the alcove she turned and held his gaze as he came nearer, just before she stepped into the alcove she curtseyed low, and rising, blew him a slow and tender kiss of profound gratitude. Seconds later, when he reached the alcove, it was completely deserted.

◆◆◆

Chapter 23
Fever

When Miranda reached home she was shivering in spite of the warmth of the day, she felt headachy and ached all over, she made herself a hot lemon and took two paracetamol. She put two bottles of water on the bedside table and drew the curtains. Alice was still away and when Miranda awoke she knew there was something badly wrong, her throat was so raspingly sore, she was dizzy and hot. She reached for the water and gratefully gulped it down, then slept again, waking with a headache so bad that she stumbled to the kitchen for more paracetamol, hardly aware of what time it was. The glands in her neck were unbearably tender and her lower back ached and ached.

She picked up the letters from behind the door on automatic pilot and had to lie down on the bed with them in her hand for half an hour before she could gather the strength to open them. Scalding tears poured down her cheeks as she read that her further study funding application had been turned down. Miranda knew the lack of her father more sharply then than at any time since he had died, why was she losing out on all her life chances when both her Mum and Dad had worked so hard to give her the opportunities to lead the peaceful academic life she longed for? She knew that the money had been there for her, that this time in her life had been planned for and looked forward to by both her parents. How had it happened that what her Mum had built up was now in the hands of someone who felt no guilt at all in depriving Miranda of what was rightfully hers? Why had her father been so stupid or did he not care about her? The King had seemed to think nothing of depriving Princess Mary of her birthright when he married again, who was to say that her Father hadn't felt the same way?

The thought of spending her working life at the mercy of people like the terrible Janet the bulldozer crushed her spirit. Her thoughts spiraled down and down, taking her to dark places where every painful thought was magnified and raw against her ill and troubled mind. How had Henry been able to go from loving her to his terrible cold indifference? Could it really have meant nothing? What if she had got it wrong when taking the message back and even now the Marchants were facing accusations of witchcraft? The thoughts became increasingly troubled and slipped into uneasy dreams where she walked down roads that were familiar from her childhood, anxiously searching for her lost mother but never finding her. Sometime in the night she knocked over the last bottle of water and when she reached for a drink there was nothing on the bedside table and she was too weak to get more. Her temperature crept up higher and her hair was wet with perspiration, she felt herself give up and there was even a relief in it.

'Miranda, wake up, wake up.' Alice's voice seemed to come from a long way away, Miranda felt her head being lifted and water splashed against her lips as Alice held the cup as steadily as she could. Miranda drank a little and fell back against the pillow, exhausted. She felt a cool cloth wiping her face and arms and heard the windows being thrown open to let some blessedly cool air into the room. Miranda sipped a little more of the water as Alice supported her head, then the damp pillow was replaced by a cool fresh one and she slipped back into sleep.

Somewhere as she drifted she could hear Alice's voice, steely determination holding back her panic as she said, 'No she is not well enough to come to the surgery, if you won't send the Doctor then I will call an ambulance and tell them that you, the receptionist, decided that the Doctor should not attend.'

Then, 'Thank you, I will do my best to keep her hydrated until then.'

Even later she became conscious of someone taking her pulse and heard a sensible voice say, 'Her temperature is a problem, I am going to give her antibiotics now and a prescription, if her temperature does not start to fall in six hours or if she isn't able to drink then we'll have to take her into hospital. Are you able to make sure she drinks every half an hour for the next few hours?'

'Yes, and I'll get the prescription.' No hesitation, even in the state she was in, Miranda felt a rush of gratitude for Alice's calm practicality.

'Right, I'll be back in six hours, I am the emergency doctor on call so if you think she is deteriorating before then, call me and I'll advise you or come out.' The door closed quietly behind the Doctor and the next few hours were a blur of being awoken every time she closed her eyes to drink water and to be helped to the bathroom. It was almost pleasant, the drifting away, then the dreadful back pains and unbearably sore glands would overwhelm her again and she longed for it to end.

In the early morning, she woke up properly for the first time, she was weak and shaky but she felt as if she was back in the world. She made her way to the bathroom and when she got back Alice was in her bedroom, 'sit on the chair for a minute Miranda while I sort out some fresh bedding, then I'll bring you some chicken soup.'

'Chicken soup for breakfast?' Miranda asked as she sat down unsteadily.

'Good to hear you say something normal, I'm afraid I wasn't going to keep the antibiotics for Henry, whoever he is!' Lemon and lavender scents filled the room as Alice shook out a fresh duvet cover. 'There you go, back into bed.'

As Alice headed for the kitchen, Miranda smiled for the first time in a long time, keep the antibiotics for Henry indeed, she definitely wasn't single minded enough, why couldn't she have feverish dreams about keeping the emeralds for herself! With Alice in charge, Miranda could almost enjoy being ill, she was weak and ate very little but she kept sipping water and later in the day sat up and had a bowl of Cornish vanilla ice cream, Alice laughed as she watched her finish it,

'All is not lost, do you think you'll be OK by yourself tomorrow? I'll make sure you've got drinks before I go and there's plenty of soup and ice cream.'

'Sounds perfect, I'll be fine' unexpected tears filled her eyes as she said, 'what would I do without you Alice?'

Alice was serious for a moment, 'would you do the same for me?'

'You know I would, in a heartbeat but you've got a battalion of sisters and cousins and they'd have to fight your Mum and Dad to get to you if you needed help!'

'Then don't say one more word about it, I am here for you, you are here for me, end of story, agreed?'

Miranda awoke next morning still weak but a little better, she fired up her laptop and took it back to bed together with the printout showing the very few details of the Marchant family, researched and printed before she had gone back to give Lord Benedict the details of the shipwreck. She couldn't help but feel excited, she knew from all her years of being enthralled with Medieval history that you could discover the most extraordinary details of the past when researching even if a thousand others had missed them; but this, to be able to see how one act reverberated down the centuries was the most curious of experiences.

It was a strange moment, after typing Lord Marchant into the search engine, her index finger hovered over the enter key for a few seconds before she tapped it firmly. There were thousands of results, literally thousands.

To say the Marchants had thrived was an understatement; over the years there were explorers, captains of business, founders of charities, Admirals and Generals, authors and artists. There was an image of one Lady Marchant leading a suffragette rally and another Lady Marchant wearing a ruby necklace that seemed to glow even in a centuries old photograph of a painting. A Lord Marchant had fallen at Waterloo and in more recent articles the current heir to the title was included in a 'most eligible bachelor' list along with royalty and technology tycoons.

Miranda smiled as she was reminded of the way the ladies at Court had vied for Lord Benedict to wear their favours at the joust, it seemed as if the Marchant family charm had continued down the line. It looked as if he worked hard to stay out of the press though, there were no clear photographs of the current heir to the title although his father had a look of an older Lord Benedict about him.

There were so many photographs of the beautiful White Hart Manor, the current Lady Marchant, Clarrissa, had carried out a massive restoration project and allowed photographers in to see the stunning results. The beautifully proportioned rooms with their almost floor to ceiling French windows were flooded with sunlight, the intense colours and rich fabrics of the curtains and carpets created a breathtaking backdrop to the walls of books, the comfortable sofas, the high-backed chairs and lovingly polished pieces of furniture and silver that had quite literally been handed down for centuries.

A flood of feeling was released in Miranda, she was so glad that she had been able to repay Benedict for saving her, it felt so right that Lady Marchant and Maria had not lost their beloved White Hart Manor.

Mixed in with this was a dreadful feeling of unfairness, why did this present day Lady Clarrissa Marchant have everything while she was struggling for just one single year's funding? Why hadn't she sorted things out when she was at Henry's Court to at least bury the Emerald necklace somewhere where she could dig it up now? Why hadn't she seen who the real prize was when she had the chance?

In theory she could go back again but even the thought of the potential danger was terrifying. Miranda tried to keep the feelings under control and just be glad that things had obviously gone right but it was hard, everyone seemed to have done well out of it except her.

In fact, she had even lost her mother's pearl necklace, Betsy had probably got her hands on that and her descendants would pop up on Antiques Roadshow any day now furiously insisting that it had been in their family for hundreds of years even though the expert was adamant that it dated only from the twentieth century. Miranda couldn't help laughing to herself at that thought, the idea of a present day Betsy popping up on television lightened her mood and she spent a fascinating few hours finding out as much as she could about the family history. There was nothing that could tell her who Lord Benedict and Maria had married though.

Miranda spent the next couple of days letting the various Supporting Artistes' agencies know that she would be available for work next week, tracking down obscure grants that could possibly fund her research and wondering whether she should give up on her dreams and try and get a proper job.

Intermittently plans on how she could use the key again and fund her future properly surfaced in her mind, maybe buying some land in what would then have been farmland and was now prime London real estate. Perhaps travelling down to White Hart Manor in 1535 and bargaining with Lady Marchant for generous compensation in return for the information on the shipwreck, although it may be that bargaining with Lord Benedict would have more compensations than just the material ones.

These reveries would end abruptly as her thoughts ended up back in the locked room with the threat of being sentenced for witchcraft hanging over her, besides there was no guaranteeing what the intervening centuries would bring and what the impact would be back in her own time.

She seemed to have made it all go pretty well for the Marchant family through the ages though she thought a little bitterly. Miranda decided to sleep on it all, there was a relief in allowing oneself to be ill, not having to make decisions just yet, even the vivid dreams had a cathartic quality about them.

◆◆◆

Chapter 24

The journey

There was maybe just the hint of a cooler morning in the air when Miranda woke up, it would be gone within half an hour but it gave the first feeling of summer passing its peak. It was pleasant to lie in bed with a breeze blowing in cooling the room and to feel some vitality returning to her mind and body.

Miranda decided to approach the idea of going back through the secret door and travelling to White Hart Manor as if she was writing a paper on it, she would research the practicalities, there was no need to make a decision yet. She researched buying historical costumes and stage jewellery that had been used in film or theatre, they were much sought after by collectors, an expensive option that would take the very last of her funds.

She was fascinated by the genuine groats and silver coins from Henry's time that were for sale on-line, to think they still existed across all these centuries, they were way out of her price range though and she was going to need to pay to travel to Wiltshire by post horse at the very least, the schoolgirl riding lessons would need to be dusted off for sure.

She puzzled over this for days, finally finding her Eureka moment as she grated some fresh ginger for a hot drink, a slow smile spreading over her face.

Miranda spent several days gathering the information and moving the pieces of the different options around in her mind, there was never an absolute moment when she made the firm decision to go back but little by little the decision was made. She ordered new vellum copies of IF, the lyrics and music of her adaptation of John Denver's masterpiece and the beautiful poem 'If you painted your life'.

The illness and the break from all the intensity had brought Miranda some hard gained perspective. Henry was not the man she had thought he was, she had mistaken gilt for gold and now she could see the tarnish clearly.

Time and time again her memories illuminated the real Tudor hero, Sir Benedict was not only a man who had risked all for her, his almost black eyes and dark hair that waved in an unruly manner at the nape of his neck kept drifting back into her mind's eye. The way he mounted his horse, with a vigour that clearly demonstrated that he was enjoying his physical prime; the practiced way he had held off the eager ladies of the Court, valuing the Marchant name too highly to allow any of the daughters of the ambitious to gain any hold over him.

To have the opportunity to meet him again was irresistible, it was possible he would see her as nothing more than a messenger, to be swiftly disregarded as soon as he knew about the shipwreck but that was a chance she was willing to take.

Eventually all was ready, Miranda packed the replica Tudor bag with a good quality day gown she had sourced from a second hand theatre costumes company. The modest cut and deep green fine cloth with matching crescent hood trimmed with seed pearls showed her to be a lady of some wealth and substance. She added the string of costume pearls that looked exactly like the real thing and the handmade calfskin shoes with the square toes, these had been the most expensive item and marked her out as being from the upper echelons of society. Her undershift was of the finest lawn and trimmed in exquisite lace. It was not much to start a whole new life but if Miranda's plans succeeded it would be enough. She added the poems and songs in the beautifully crafted reproduction book and left the flat with only enough cash to get to Greenwich.

Miranda experienced a real pang of sorrow when she left the letter for Alice telling her that she needed time by herself and asking her to find someone else to share the flat if she hadn't let contacted her within a fortnight. It did seem hard on Alice but Miranda needed to put herself first now, there was too much at stake.

Lastly Miranda filled every in inch of remaining space in her travelling bag with what she needed to make her way in 1535, this was in addition to what she had carefully sewn into the wide false hem of her dress, it should be enough.

As usual the Old Royal Naval College at Greenwich had many visitors, people moved about in small groups and you could nearly always tell which were fascinated by the naval history and which sought out the clues of its Tudor past.

It was the work of a moment to reach the alcove unseen and she changed into her Tudor gown in the cool and dim light. She pushed her clothes beneath the stone bench into the darkest recess, they would surely be found at some point but there was nothing to identify her.

She took a few deep breaths and then sat down on the bench to try and keep the sensations as stable as possible, she put the secret key on the fine chain around her neck into the lock. When the room stopped spinning, Miranda sat in absolute silence and listened to the sounds of the masked ball while she regained her composure and checked that all was well with her precious bag. Then she rose, straightened her gown and stood tall before stepping out.

◆◆◆

Chapter 25
The road to White Hart Manor

Miranda kept to the shadows of the Great Hall, deliberately not looking directly at the dancers as they bowed and whirled in the lights of hundreds of candles and lamps, their jewels glistening as they moved. Out of the corner of her eye she could see The King in his golden mask making his bow to the lady in the sapphire and silver mask and knew that Jane Seymour's story was being written in this future. She could also see the fine figure of Lord Benedict and she was shocked to feel her heart give a bump at the fleeting glimpse of his handsome profile. She swept quickly through the side door, determined to avoid being noticed by any of the dancers.

'Boy, come here!' the messenger approached her obediently and bowed, awaiting his orders. 'Take a message to Betsy Grimshaw, the lady's maid. You know her?' Miranda knew well of the effectiveness of the Palace servants' network and she was not surprised when he nodded. 'Tell her I wish to speak privately with her, I will sit in the quiet recess there, do you see it?'

'Yes My Lady' he set off smartly, the lady hadn't given him anything for taking the message and he knew full well he would get short shrift if he expected a tip from Betsy but he didn't want to feel the rough side of her tongue either. 'Who is it?' Betsy hurriedly wiped her hands and tidied her hair under her cap as best she could. 'Well what does she look like?' In the face of his mute shrugs she could only scold the lad under her breath as she followed him at a brisk pace back to the side hall.

'You asked for me Your Ladyship?' Betsy curtseyed low, she didn't know the lady.

'Hello Betsy, we haven't met but you have been spoken of most warmly by a friend of the lady you served who has retreated to the convent. My name is Mistress Miranda Glover.' Miranda's smile was completely genuine, it was so good to see Betsy again!

'Thank you Mistress.' Betsy blushed, it was rare to be spoken to so kindly by a Lady, never mind given compliments.

'Yes, she tells me that you are a capable and sensible woman who can be relied upon. I have need of such a person for a few weeks.'

Betsy was startled, 'do you need a lady's maid while you are at Court Mistress?'

'Not exactly Betsy, I need someone to make some arrangements for me and then to travel with me to Wiltshire as my maid, certainly for a few weeks, possibly for longer.'

'Arrangements? Wiltshire?' Betsy was cautious, this lady had appeared from nowhere and needed 'arrangements' what could she mean?

'I have no money but I have goods of value, I would seek the right person to make some trades to enable me to travel to Wiltshire, purchase some gowns and enable me to pay you well. Are you that person Betsy?'

'I - I think so' Betsy was still a little taken aback at the sudden change in her circumstances but she was certainly interested in the idea of being paid well although the thought of leaving London was unsettling. 'What goods do you have to trade?' She looked around but Miranda had chosen well and there was no-one within earshot.

Miranda opened her hand and showed Betsy the fat knobs of ginger root that had been loosely wrapped in a plain cotton square, Betsy breathed in sharply, 'Oh my, Mrs Williams keeps that under lock and key!'

Miranda smiled and opened her other hand to show two sizeable curls of cinnamon, 'Can you could get a good price for me Betsy? I know very well that you are trustworthy and would not cheat me but I do not know if you are able to get the right price yourself.'

Betsy felt on firmer ground now, her mind was totting up values and thinking about the people she needed to talk to 'I'll get a good price, it will cause too many questions if Mrs Williams knows so I will need to go into the city. Where shall I come to you Mistress?'

'I need somewhere to stay until we travel to Wiltshire Betsy, can you arrange it?'

'I will find you comfortable lodgings before I see to business. Please stay here a little longer Mistress and I will return for you.'

Miranda sat quietly, the music of the ball drifted through to her and she recognized the melodies of the dances she had shared with Henry, she was experiencing a peculiar state of mind, her heart was thundering with the excitement of carrying out her plans but she was also feeling a profound calm, as if she was on a path that was leading her the right way.

In a very short time Betsy returned wearing a woolen cloak and carrying an elegant heavy silk cloak for Miranda, 'My Lady left some items behind and graciously gave me leave to use them Mistress' Miranda smiled her thanks and rose to allow Betsy to arrange the deep rose cloak around her shoulders, even though it was a warm night she raised the hood of the cloak so that her face was shadowed. Accompanied by a male servant bid by Betsy, they left the Palace and walked down to the river's edge through the palace grounds. The grounds were well lit by lamps and drifts of evening conversation reached them from hidden places in the gardens. The river boats were vying for position, they stepped into a small boat and the taciturn boatman set off down the river. Betsy handed the boatman some coins as they stepped from the riverboat into the warm night of the city and he grunted his acknowledgment.

They walked silently through prosperous looking streets and the dwindling light, passing unacknowledged amongst the respectable townspeople taking their evening walk until they reached a fine half timbered house with lights burning in the downstairs windows. The landlady of the dwelling assured Betsy that they did indeed have comfortable lodgings available and she welcomed Miranda and Betsy inside. Miranda followed the housekeeper up the well lit wooden stairs with an intricately carved bannister, the scent of lavender and beeswax mingled with the aroma of baking coming from the back kitchen.

The two rooms were well furnished, one had an elegant upholstered chair with a cushion embroidered with wild flowers, a good oak table with two plain stools was positioned alongside the tall window to allow a good view of the broad street while dining. The sleeping chamber had a high and comfortable bed with a washstand, jug and bowl and a wide bench. When the housekeeper drew back the bedcover to proudly display spotless sheets strewn with dried lavender a delicious scent filled the room and with relief Miranda agreed to take the rooms for two nights and to pay extra for beeswax candles.

Betsy asked the housekeeper to arrange for some warm ale, bread and pottage and then helped Miranda off with her cloak and shoes when the woman left the room to set the maid about her duties. 'I will return as soon as I have made the trade Mistress Glover. I will do my very best to get a good price. It will likely be the morrow before I return.' Betsy was proud of the trust being placed in her honesty and in her abilities, she had selected expensive lodgings where visitors to the Palace often stayed.

'Thank you Betsy, once we have ready funds we can arrange the journey to Wiltshire, I hope you will accompany me.'

'I will tell them at the Palace that my mother needs me at home and that I must go for some weeks, they will be cross but will release me.' Betsy didn't have many chances for adventure and had never travelled outside London, her initial caution was giving way to excitement now. 'I will tell the housekeeper to bring you warm water and fresh washing cloths Mistress, she is a goodly soul and her lodgings are in demand, you will fare well here until I come back.'

When Betsy had gone, Miranda made herself comfortable and checked the remaining ginger roots, nutmegs, cinnamon curls and securely wrapped packages of purest sugar in her bag; over a hundred nutmegs tapped against her ankles whenever she ruffled the hem of her gown, sewn into the extra wide false hem, they would not see the light of the day until the circumstances were exactly right. Betsy could not possibly trade items of such vast value but Miranda knew very well who could. Miranda slept well and was enjoying a late breakfast of a baked mutton pie when Betsy returned. Her wide face was flushed with excitement as she poured the purse of silver coins out on to the table. 'Enough for lodgings, gowns, the journey and with plenty left over Mistress!'.

◆◆◆

Chapter 26
The negotiations

Lady Marchant stood back a little from the huge windows that gave out onto the stone balustrades of the Manor, observing the small party as their horses passed through the young copper beech avenue. The young lady mounted on a proud stepping mare was attended by an alert manservant who handled his own horse with bred in the bone ease. A little further back along the avenue a respectable looking maidservant was sitting alongside the driver of a cart. The visitor was not known to Lady Marchant and she watched with interest as they came nearer.

When her manservant tapped at the heavy oak door of the drawing room to inform her that a Mistress Glover requested an audience with Lady Marchant she had already watched the travelling party dismount and had looked in vain for any identifying livery.

'I will see her'

Her manservant bowed and ten minutes later Miranda curtseyed low to Lady Marchant. She was nervous, she knew well that Lady Marchant would be suspicious of an approach from someone with no introductions and that the next few minutes were crucial. At the same time she felt such a rush of recognition and affection, even Lady Marchant's demeanour as Lady of the Manor, Matriarch of the Marchant family, could not dampen down the absolute pleasure she felt at being in her company again.

Lady Marchant warmed a little towards the graceful girl, besides the days were long and largely uneventful at White Hart Manor, an unknown visitor certainly added interest. She could see that the worst of the travel dust had been cleaned from Mistress Glover's cloak and shoes, the Manor's household servants had obviously looked after her. No doubt they were currently offering hospitality to Mistress Glover's servants, eager to trade fresh pies and cool ale to find out what her business with Lady Marchant was.

'Be seated Mistress Glover, I understand that you wish to talk to me.'

'Thank you Lady Marchant, yes I would have some confidential conversation with you, you are very kind to see me.'

Conversation ceased while the servant poured spiced wine and laid out some fresh baked scones with golden butter that had been churned in the Manor dairy, there were tiny latticed tarts too, bursting with strawberries, gooseberries and redcurrants from the bountiful kitchen gardens. The silver goblets and plate graced the low oak table, burnished with a daily polishing of beeswax. The elegance of the room, the comfort of the furnishings and the food and drink all created a feeling of rest, of homecoming, of peace. Miranda knew Lady Marchant too well to take anything for granted though.

'Lady Marchant, I have come by some knowledge which I believe will be beneficial to your family. In return I would seek your help, I have items of value I wish to sell but no money and no family to protect me. If the knowledge I would share with you is as valuable to you as I believe it to be, will you help me?'

There was silence in the room, Miranda's hand shook as she sipped her wine and picked up a redcurrant tart, the activities covering her nervousness as she waited for Lady Marchant to respond. She bit into the mouth watering pastry and felt the tart flavor of the fruit flood her taste buds, even at such a tense moment she had to resist the temptation to pop it into her mouth whole and pick up another.

'let me be clear Mistress Glover, you declare that you have knowledge that will be useful to me even though I have never heard of you and have no idea how you come to know me or to be here. You also seem to be asking me to act as your guardian, again rather surprising when I did not know of your existence until fifteen minutes ago. A rather unusual opening to an acquaintance.'

Miranda met Lady Marchant's gaze steadily, 'Indeed, you are correct on all counts Your Ladyship, I also do not know whether you will then keep to your side of the bargain, it will be entirely within your power to hear my information and then refuse to help me.'

'So why trust me?' Lady Marchant's voice was sharp, she recognized a kindred strong mind and dropped the pretence of one lady entertaining another.

'I know your reputation at Court, if you say that you will help me if my information is of value then you will. Lady Marchant's word can be relied upon. I also know that I will get short shrift if I have wasted your time.' There was silence, a long one, Lady Marchant was not to be taken in by flattery but she liked this description of herself. 'How come you to know of Court doings?' she was wary but curious.

'People love to talk of gossip from the Court, I do not claim to know more than that.'

'And how came you by information that can benefit the Marchants?'

'Before my father died he had travelled much to many lands and had seagoing acquaintances, he was recently in the company of one who passed this information to him on his deathbed, my father was stricken by the same illness within days and left the knowledge of the man's last conversation to me in a letter, I did not have the chance to speak with him again. This was three weeks ago.'

'Three weeks ago! Pray what sickness was this?' Miranda understood Lady Marchant's fear, the sickness that swept whole villages and cities could take a life between daybreak and nightfall when all had been well on waking.

'It was the sleeping sickness Lady Marchant. I was not with my father after he contracted it, you need have no fears that I have brought it with me.'

Lady Marchant looked relieved, 'I am sorry for your loss Mistress Glover, you must miss him sorely.' Miranda could be completely genuine now, 'With all my heart, I know what it is to feel alone in the world.' This silence was more comfortable.

Then Lady Marchant spoke quite gently, 'My dear, I understand that you and your father may think that your information is valuable to us, if it is I will pay its worth but please prepare yourself to find that it is not. I will speak truth but it may not be a truth you like to hear.'

'I have perfect faith in your judgement as to value Lady Marchant, if my father was wrong he made his error in good faith and it will not lessen what he tried to do for me' Miranda bowed her head to Lady Marchant and was rewarded with a corresponding nod. In silence, she produced the carefully crafted letter that contained the description and co-ordinates of the shipwreck of the White Hart. Lady Marchant's colour passed to parchment white in seconds, even her great composure could not hide all traces of the shock.

When she could speak, she said, 'You understand what this means?'

'I do' Miranda longed to help Lady Marchant to some wine but she did not dare, this was not yet the Lady Marchant who knew and trusted Miranda.

'I will send for my grandson, in the meantime you will be my welcome guest, decisions on whether this is valuable information or not cannot yet be made.' Lady Marchant rang the bell and instructed the servant to tell the housekeeper that Mistress Glover would be their guest until further notice. 'I think you may enjoy walking in the gardens until your room is ready Miss Glover.' Miranda recognized a dismissal when she heard it, she curtseyed and followed the servant from the room.

◆◆◆

Chapter 27
Lord Benedict

Miranda awoke when the morning sun was well risen, Betsy was moving silently in the room, laying out her gown, this was a new one, a paneled day gown of russet silk. It was matched with a fuller hood than the pretty pearl crescents, not an unflattering gable but certainly modest and respectable. It framed Miranda's beautiful face perfectly, the fabric of the dress was light and moved becomingly as Miranda walked. Maria drank in every detail as she sat across the table from Miranda and broke her fast in company with their guest.

'and will my brother come alone or bring guests Grandmother?' Maria's longing for young company and some excitement was evident, many girls of fourteen from aristocratic families were married at Maria's age, often with a year or two of dancing and entertainments at Court already behind them.

'He will come alone this time Maria, I hope that you will keep our guest entertained until he arrives? Likely it will be late in the afternoon.'

Lady Marchant knew that she needed to be more open with Maria at some point, the Court had become a dangerous place since Queen Katherine's crown had unbelievably been toppled, it had seemed wise to keep the pretty young Maria safely at home. From all accounts the King's eye was wandering again and Anne Boleyn would stop at literally nothing to defeat her enemies. Better to be bored than come to the notice of either of the royal pair. Fortunately, the Howards and Seymours were so determined to throw their daughters into the fray that, so far, Lady Marchant's one precious granddaughter had not been called to be a lady-in-waiting.

'With the greatest pleasure!' Maria bowed her head in acknowledgement to Miranda and soon they walked amongst the cool woodland to the west of the Manor. It was a pretty walk and Maria pointed out where her Grandfather had built the various garden features to catch the sun at different times of the day. It conjured up a picture of the young Lord and Lady Marchant planning for the future and for their family for generations, building a home that would stand the test of time and welcome home many a weary warrior for centuries to come.

Maria was disappointed when she realised that Miranda had never been at Court, she shared her longing to go there and her frustrations at living such a quiet life in the country. They had turned to head back to the Manor as the day's heat was rising when they saw a magnificent horse being ridden at full speed through the copper beech tree avenue. Even at this distance Miranda recognized Lord Benedict, his mastery of the beautiful animal and the way his vibrant energy showed as he rode would have been enough but his manly profile and dark hair confirmed it. Miranda's body seemed to know it before her mind acknowledged it, she felt almost weak and breathless, overcome by seeing him again.

'Come, it is my brother, he is early!' Maria started off at a pace that was hard to keep up with, Lord Benedict neither saw them not heard Maria's cries, he brought the horse to a halt at the stone staircase that fanned out beneath the enormous oak front door and threw the reins to a groom that had emerged at a run.

'Cool him down!'

Lord Benedict took the stone steps two at a time, shouting for his grandmother as he gained the hall. By the time Maria and Miranda reached the Manor, Lady Marchant and Lord Benedict were behind the locked door of her small private parlour, the huge windows to the terrace were closed and locked too, not a sound could be heard. Maria stopped uncertainly before the door, Miranda stopped too,

'Maybe we should wait until your grandmother sends for us?'

'Yes, let us walk in the gallery, I will show you the paintings of my Grandfather and my Mama and Papa, Benedict has been painted too, it will be my turn this autumn.'

'And your grandmother?'   Maria smiled and led Miranda to a painting, Miranda had been expecting to see Lady Marchant as she was now, a commanding figure, the matriarch of the Marchants. But this was a beautiful young woman of maybe two and twenty, her flawless skin and welcoming smile showing the happiness of a bride and a mother. 'My Grandfather ordered this painting as a thank you to my Grandmother for giving him the Marchant heir, my father. Grandmother was a renowned beauty of the Court, she had many admirers before her father accepted the suit of Lord Marchant.'

They moved on to look at the other portraits, Maria was not sad when she looked at her mother and father, she had no memories of them, her brother and Grandmother had been all to her from her earliest days. As they stopped in front of the portrait of Lord Benedict the door below was flung open and a shout echoed up into the gallery,

'Where is Mistress Glover? Bring her to me now!' Maria was most shocked, 'What can my brother be shouting like that for? Let us make haste Mistress Miranda.'

They hurried towards the beautiful oak stairs and Lord Benedict caught his first glimpse of Miranda as tendrils of her golden caramel hair escaped her hood as she gathered the skirts of the russet dress and almost ran down the stairs, for a few seconds Lord Benedict was disconcerted by the unexpected sight of exquisite ankles clad in silk stockings, he had to force himself to raise his eyes upwards and saw that all other aspects of the unknown lady were just as pleasing.

◆◆◆

Chapter 28
Passion rising

Lord Benedict's preparations were underway; he would leave at sunrise the next day with Blackstone, his man of business. Maria and his Grandmother delighted in ordering a supper to especially please him that evening, it was so good to have him at home at White Hart Manor and it felt like a celebration even though all tried to stay cautious. The duck was perfect, cooked slowly in a plum sauce exactly as he liked it. The summer berry tartlets were delicious, the cream fresh and thick, the wine was deep and sensuous. Every morsel of food had come from the Marchant's own Manor lands and farms, it was a good feeling.

Lord Benedict's good mood improved with every course and whenever he glanced appreciatively at Miranda he was sometimes quick enough to see her glance away, she blushed, he smiled, Lady Marchant took note. Lord Benedict's initial suspicion of Miranda's story had lessened when he had talked to her; now he believed that if she was wrong it was done in good faith, and the thought that she could be right! That his fortunes could be restored and even increased. He would have ridden out that night if he could but good sense and a care for the horses prevailed.

Now he enjoyed finding out more about Miranda, when the company realised that she could play and sing they pressed her to entertain them, she was a little apprehensive but the time she had spent practicing at Henry's Court served her well. After she had sung a familiar song while Maria played the virginal she decided to make a huge impact, she was playing for high stakes and the time felt right. Excusing herself for a few minutes she fetched the music and lyrics from her room and taking her seat at the virginal she watched their astonished faces as they heard John Denver's beautiful opening lines for the very first time, she could ask for nothing more than their rapt attention from 'You fill up my senses' to the very last closing note.

Lady Marchant wanted to know much more about Miranda, she gained her promise to show her more of her poetry and music on the next day. Miranda helped Maria start to learn the notes so that she could play the music herself. It felt rather wonderful to be at the centre of the Marchant family's attention, any worries about whether she deserved it were swiftly and rigorously batted away, she hadn't written the song but she had used her ingenuity to bring it to the sixteenth century and she was going to enjoy the moment! Lord Benedict's sly glances had given way to open admiration during her singing.

As the evening closed in the lamps were lit, after one more glass of the delicious and potent wine, Lord Benedict asked Miranda if she would walk in the gardens with him, he would like to ask her a little more about the seafaring man her father had known. They walked and she gladly took the arm he offered, the summer evening scents of columbine and honeysuckle combined to hang heavy in the air and on the senses. As they rounded a corner of a walled garden where the stones of the wall were warmed through by the summer's heat and there were no lamps to directly light that sheltered spot, suddenly, without any warning, he pushed her up against the warm wall and held her firmly by the wrists against the roughhewn stone. His lips sought hers greedily, the tension of the last hours, the heat of the night and the disinhibiting effect of a little too much wine pushing aside any thoughts of decorum.

'Tell me you don't want me and I'll let you go' his voice was harsh with longing, his dark eyes held hers in a passionate lock, reflecting the desire that was surging up inside her.

She felt the blood rise in her body as she responded to his questing kiss.

At that very moment Lady Marchant's voice called to Lord Benedict; she was literally feet away and they sprang apart as she entered the walled garden, with Maria at her side. 'Really Benedict, you must not keep Mistress Glover in the cool air, she may catch a chill, come my dear Mistress Glover, give me your arm and we will return to the house.'

Benedict and Miranda spoke no more that evening. As he drifted into sleep his mind played out the rest of the evening had it been without interruption and Miranda's dreams were no less disturbed as she imagined his kisses becoming more and more insistent. In his dreams, he pulled up her dress and she did not resist, she wanted him. She dreamt that she twisted her hands into his hair pulling his mouth towards her again, greedy for everything he had to give, while he held her hard against him by the buttocks. He pulled up her dress and under shift and she felt his hands start to explore the nakedness of the firm, ripe peaches of her buttocks, both of them were panting and small groans were escaping him.

Who knew who had dreamt what in that fevered night? Even the scent of the lavender crushed heedlessly beneath their frantic bodies found its way into the dreaming. In the morning, they were both as exhausted as if they had spent the whole night together in reality.

◆◆◆

Chapter 29
The shipwreck

Every thought at White Hart Manor was with Lord Benedict as he journeyed to Sheerness and met with the men who would prove the truth, or not, of Miranda's message. Although Lady Marchant encouraged Miranda and Maria to practice at the virginal while she carefully checked the household accounts, this outward veneer of a normal day did little to dispel the reality that every ear was waiting for the sound of hooves.

When Lady Marchant could bear it no longer she instructed Maria and Miranda to prepare themselves to walk in the gardens. When they reached the limit of the beautiful formal walks she pressed on beyond the bowers of apple and pear trees and struck out for the park and even beyond that to the woodland. Her pace meant that Maria and Miranda had to step lively to keep up. Seeing the intensity of her strides, Miranda could see how Lady Marchant was burning up inside, how the thought of losing White Hart Manor, of losing Maria's marriage chances and Benedict's position in life was powering an inner turmoil that would never reach her lips.

As they walked, Miranda caught a glimpse of a familiar dress whisking away through the woodland. She hesitated, uncertain of whether she should mention what she had seen.

Lady Marchant missed nothing though, 'It seems that your maid is finding the benefits of good country air to be quite invigorating.'

Miranda glanced sharply at her, 'and it seems that your household is making her feel very welcome.' Maria snorted with laughter, Betsy and the under footman had to break cover to dash towards the house and it was plain to see that they were hand clasped. The mood lightened as for the first time Lady Marchant seemed less consumed by her thoughts and was amused by the interruption.

'Ah well, if events turn as we hope and you stay with us longer Mistress Miranda at least you will not have a sulky maid to sour your mornings.'

Miranda noted the use of her first name and felt warmed by it, 'but will I have a broken hearted one Your Ladyship? Is Betsy's beau a true one?'

'He has no wife and I know nothing against his character, it may be timely to talk to your maid though, remind her that it's always the woman who must be wise in these matters or pay the price.'

Miranda nodded, it was almost a small bow, both women knew whom the conversation was really about. As they turned back towards the house, they saw a messenger gallop up the Copper Beech avenue, the horse flecked with sweat, testament to the speed at which it had travelled. Once again Lady Marchant's pace left Maria and Miranda rushing to keep up. They were spared the whole breathless rush though as they saw the messenger throw himself from his horse, speak to the groom and then set off across the immense sweep of lawn towards the party.

He threw himself down on one knee, 'Your Ladyship' he gasped. 'Give me the message!' Lady Marchant held out her hand impatiently as the exhausted man hesitated. 'His Lordship was most insistent that you should be completely alone to receive the message Your Ladyship.'

'Leave me!'

Miranda and Maria, did not stop to curtsey, this moment was beyond etiquette. They headed off towards the house and a few minutes later they observed the messenger following in their wake.

With trembling hands, Lady Marchant undid the bulky package, a large jagged square of dull deep-red rolled into her hand, the message was brief,

'My Dear Grandmother,

This ruby is just the beginning, White Hart Manor is saved. Be circumspect in what you tell my sister and our guest until I return,

Benedict.'

Lady Marchant quickly rewrapped the package, her hands shook and her heart beat faster, she struck out across the lawn towards her beloved White Hart Manor, smiling as she saw Miranda and Maria at the window of the drawing room, peering anxiously towards her.

'What has he found? When will he be back? Can we go there?' Maria's questions tumbled over each other, there was no opportunity for her Grandmother to answer them,

'Hush Maria, it seems that things may go well for the Marchants, for the details we must wait until there is more from your brother, your patience will not be tried long I am sure.'

Later, Lady Marchant found the opportunity for private conversation with Miranda. 'You will not find the Marchant Family ungrateful if all goes well Mistress Miranda, have you thought of your future?'

'I have Lady Marchant, I would like a modest establishment of my own, to be my own mistress on my own lands. I would also seek your ongoing friendship, as you know I am alone in the world' Miranda hesitated a moment, 'I have other valuables that I would trade to add to whatever generosity you show me, it may be that I will need a man of business.'

Lady Marchant was intrigued, 'may I know what form these valuables take?   It may be that Blackstone can act for you, however it may be well if he thinks he is acting for me.'

Miranda hesitated longer this time, then 'If you will excuse me for some little time I will show you.'

She swept a low curtsey and left the room. She knew Lady Marchant to be trustworthy, even so she would be circumspect, her experience with Henry had taught her that things can change and take a dark turn in the blink of an eye. She selected one curl of cinnamon, a generous wrap of sugar and two nutmegs. She was well aware that the value of nutmegs would rise to even more astounding levels over the coming years and she would make sure that her hidden store would be moved from the hem of her dress to an airtight place soon. She wrapped all in an embroidered cloth and returned to the drawing room,

'I would ask that we are not interrupted Your Ladyship.'

Lady Marchant was genuinely intrigued now, she rang the bell and they waited in silence until the servant appeared, 'We are not to be disturbed Roberts.'   He bowed low and left the room.

Miranda crossed to the polished oak table and moved the candlesticks, she carefully unrolled the embroidered cloth to show first the cinnamon curl, a rare smile spread across Lady Marchant's face, this was riches indeed. With a sense of occasion Miranda next revealed the startlingly white contents of the wrap,

'May I?' at Miranda's nod Lady Marchant dipped a little finger into the package, her incredulous expression as she tasted the incomparable sweetness of the pure cane sugar was really something to see, this was literally beyond what she had known existed. Then Miranda peeled back the last fold of the cloth to show the perfect nutmegs, lying side by side like jewels.

Lady Marchant literally gasped, 'do you know what you have here?'

Miranda smiled, 'I do'.

Lady Marchant's keen mind was at work now, 'Do you have more?'

Miranda hesitated yet again, she must look to her future now. 'That will depend on the price I get for these.' She looked fearlessly at Lady Marchant, she knew that she could never have spoken like this only a short time before but much had happened since then, this was a Miranda that had come into her own and she would demand that her worth was acknowledged.

'If you will entrust this to me I will speak to Blackstone as soon as he returns.'

'With all my heart My Lady, the sugar however, is a gift from me to you, I have more I can sell.'

It was rare that Lady Marchant was quite overwhelmed but this was one of those moments. She later felt an excitement that was at odds with her nature when she summoned the cook to consult on potential delicacies. The cook was no less astonished than Lady Marchant and her ideas for sweets, cakes and puddings tumbled over each other. With great ceremony, Lady Marchant and Cook locked the sugar in the kitchen cabinet and cook was entrusted with the key. Even that good woman though could not resist opening it at 5.00am the next morning and tasting just a few heavenly grains with the tip of her finger.

◆◆◆

Chapter 30

Willow House

It was more than a week before Lord Benedict returned. He was exhausted, he had stood shoulder to shoulder night and day with the men who had worked tirelessly to salvage the contents of the ship. Blackstone too was weary, he had accounted for every item, not a pearl, gold coin or ruby had been missed. The inventory had grown hour by hour until even the most cautious of men knew that the Marchant fortune had been multiplied many times over.

Notwithstanding the weariness, Blackstone went immediately to the homes of the drowned, to make secure their futures as well as to tell them their husbands, brothers and fathers were never coming home. It was sombre work but neither Lord Marchant nor Blackstone would rest until it was done.

Nothing could dim the elation though, the Marchants were jubilant and even though there were many private conversations between Lady Marchant and Lord Benedict there were many more where Benedict regaled Maria and Miranda with the moments where fresh treasures had been brought up from the holds and on one occasion he opened a package and scattered enormous pearls across the table that bounced and rolled to a breathtakingly beautiful halt in the candlelight.

Benedict's spirits were high and although he always looked happy to be in Miranda's company there were no secret looks or stolen kisses. Lady Marchant started to scold Maria for any breaches of etiquette and began more than one sentence with, 'When you are married…'

Benedict smiled affectionately, he knew that his grandmother's marriage plans had undergone a considerable boost and that she positively relished the negotiations to come which would secure the best possible husband for her beautiful Maria.

Both Lord Benedict and Lady Marchant were present when they formally thanked Miranda for leading them to the sunken ship. Lady Marchant proposed that Miranda should have the tenancy of a house on the estate for her lifetime or until she married as a reward; the friendship of the Marchants was also hers for a lifetime and Lady Marchant would introduce her to suitable society under her protection. They were taken aback when Miranda thanked them and then proposed that she should be able to continue the lease if she married and also to buy the leasehold of the house for her descendants beyond her lifetime.

Although Benedict was acquainted with the fact that her trades would make her wealthy in her own right he was amazed and somewhat impressed when she negotiated the lease in perpetuity in exchange for a portion of her tradable valuables. Miranda was well aware of how much the value of her nutmegs would soar in the years to come and she knew she was well provided for as long as she kept some back and kept them preserved from the air.

They arranged for the whole party to walk to Willow House the next day, some two miles distance from the Manor. Miranda slept fitfully that night, the excitement about the house and realizing that she really could make a whole new life for herself in this time was mixed in with her feelings about kissing Benedict, it was as if it had never happened. She understood him being caught up with the salvage operation and the huge impact it had on his life but had it really meant nothing to him? Did she want to be here if Lord

Benedict did not love her in this version of time? Could she live with that and see him marry one day with a tranquil heart?

Walking to Willow House was the most charming way to begin the day; the servants followed discreetly with refreshments in case Lady Marchant should be wearied and the warming day lifted the spirits of all. They crossed the great meadow and then walked along the prettiest of lanes where summer pinks, reds and whites nodded from the hedgerows and sharp shots of yellow peeped out from under glossy leaves.

The scent of the wild garlic refreshed their senses and Miranda listened eagerly as Lord Benedict and Lady Marchant explained that the house had been tenanted until recently and was in good repair. Maria forgot that she was a grown up lady now and seizing Miranda's hand as eagerly as any child she said, 'I could walk to you every day, we should be such friends!' Miranda laughed and agreed that would make her very happy indeed, she felt almost afraid to be so happy, what if the house was a disappointing tumbledown cottage?

As they reached the end of the lane Miranda saw the whole view of the house before her. She felt her throat constrict, she was thunderstruck. This was how she had heard people talk of love at first sight, she had never believed in it until this moment. The house was alongside a fast running stream; the willow that gave the house its name flowed gracefully over the dappled silver water, its beautiful leaves clothing the tree with a living skirt of vibrant green.

The house was no cottage, the handsome dark red brick and half timber dwelling with its latticed windows spoke of wealth and comfort. The huge solid oak front door led into a magnificent hall with a gleaming oak staircase. The enormous kitchen showed clearly that a large staff would create wonderful meals there and the well stocked kitchen garden was bursting with all manner of fruits, berries and vegetables. Miranda was surprised to see that the henhouse was home to many fat contented hens but it was quite in keeping with Lady Marchant's pragmatism to make good use of all productive land.

Miranda felt her heart swell, there was something about Willow House that said home in a way that had eluded her for many years. Even though she had understood Lady Marchant's fierce attachment to White Hart Manor she had never felt such a thing herself until this moment. Something moved in her and she knew that, with or without Lord Marchant, she was home.

They spent a happy hour exploring and Lady Marchant looked hard for any slips in housekeeping to scold the servants with but all was in order, the Marchants ran a tight ship and those who served them prided themselves on their high standards. The windows were spotless, the beautiful inlaid wooden floors gleamed, the pretty fabric of the window seats was as fresh as if it had been sewn yesterday. The huge four poster bed was not made up but fresh bed linen sprigged with dried lavender was laid across it. The sunshine warmed it every day and the lazy lavender scent drifted through the room even when there was no-one there to see.

Miranda felt as if she would like to stand on the doorstep and wave goodbye to the others, closing the door and knowing that her home was hers to shelter and protect her for all her days to come.

Lady Marchant was well pleased with Miranda's happiness with the house, she knew that their agreement would mean an enduring relationship between Miranda and the Marchants and she was not averse to the idea. A charming and sensible neighbor was an agreeable asset. Mistress Miranda would soon get over any nonsense about any affection towards Benedict, now that the family fortunes were restored he could have his pick of titled and wealthy ladies and Lady Marchant intended to put all her energies into this endeavor.

Lady Marchant insisted that Maria and Miranda rest after the mornings exertions and a light meal on their return but Miranda could not sleep, she re-arranged rooms in her mind and anxiously counted servant numbers. Above all she must be sure to tempt Betsy to stay with her, if only she would not fret for the bustle of London, Miranda could only hope that Betsy's beau was more of a draw than working and living at Court.

It was a merry group that gathered together for dinner that evening. Willow House and Lord Benedict's return to the shipwreck salvage operation the next day were the topics of conversation and all had plenty of ideas to offer while they enjoyed a delicious dish of roast partridge, cooked slowly in a rich apricot sauce. When the savouries were done, Lord Benedict's astonishment at the exquisite taste and appearance of the delicate marzipan sweetmeats created with some of the sugar Miranda had given to Lady Marchant could not but delight all who had a hand in bringing them to table. As they rose from table and left the room Lord Benedict whispered quietly that he would walk with Miranda in the small orchard at dawn if she was so inclined. Her smile as she curtseyed goodnight signaled her agreement and there could not have been a happier household in England that slept under the roof of White Hart Manor that night.

◆◆◆

Chapter 31

Honour and anger

Miranda slipped down the stairs before even Betsy was astir, she had dressed herself in a new gown, a delicate primrose silk, the bodice and sleeves edged with seed pearls sewn in the shape of daisies. Her crescent cap was trimmed in the same way and her beautiful caramel gold hair was loosely braided. Lord Benedict caught his breath as she came into sight, she seemed to bring the promise of the new day with her. Without a word, he bowed low, he looked a boy today, his happiness bringing a glow to his features and his immaculate loose white shirt and burgundy jerkin lending an informality to his appearance. He raised Miranda from her curtsey and offering her his arm they strolled through the orchard where blossom added to the beauty of the daybreak.

Eventually Lord Benedict broke the peaceful silence, 'May I ask if I would be foolish to believe that you look favourably upon me Mistress Miranda? Forgive me being forward but as you know I leave today and I do not know when I will return.'

Miranda looked up at his handsome face, 'You would not be foolish my Lord,'

He took both her hands in his and very gently raised one to his lips and kissed it. Then still very gently he leaned forward and kissed her lips softly, the sensation was felt by both, a tremor passing through their bodies and linking their hearts. Quietly they walked on, he picked a large long stemmed daisy and tucked it into her hair alongside the pearls, she smiled and the touch of his arm beneath her fingertips gave her the strangest feeling.

At last he spoke, 'I will visit you often, I will count Willow House as my second home, I will make sure you want for nothing.'

Miranda smiled at first, then looked puzzled as she tried to absorb the meaning of his words.

He continued, 'Willow House was built for my Father's mistress, he wanted her near at all times. As I do you.'

Miranda's face flushed crimson, did he really mean what she was taking from his words? Her voice was dangerously controlled when she responded, 'Let me be sure I understand you My Lord, your intention is that I should not only take up the position of your mistress in residence at Willow House, but that I should first save you from ruin and then pay your family generously for that privilege?'

There was a silence, for once Lord Benedict looked disconcerted, the situation was indeed as Miranda had described it. 'Let me be clear My Lord, it seems that you do not countenance me as a wife, I do not countenance myself as a mistress. I asked you and your family for friendship as I am alone in the world and you have offered me dishonour, I do not think there is anything more to be said.' Miranda swept him a furious curtsey and turned back towards the house. Anger drove her pace and she was shocked when he laid a hasty hand upon her shoulder to abruptly halt her progress.

'Madam!' his own shock had turned to anger, 'You are of lowly birth and my offer was indeed honourable, to be the Mistress of a Marchant has always bestowed its own status, indeed my father's Mistress kept a very fine household!'

'Indeed, and did your mother receive her?' There was silence. 'I thought not' Miranda turned away but stopped at a sudden thought. 'And do you now still intend to honour your offer to reward me for leading you to your ship?'

Lord Benedict was white with anger, 'You dare doubt my word Madam? You dare? And be sure that news of the shipwreck would have reached me eventually, the Marchant family fortune would not have been lost!' He set off at a tremendous pace towards the Manor, leaving Miranda far behind and her fury overcame her and she shouted, 'No, it would never have been found if not for me!' His anger was immense, if she had been a man he would have struck her.

He slammed into the Manor, striding past Maria and the servants, none of whom dared to say a word. Miranda returned some minutes after him with equal fury, she ran past Maria and up the staircase to her room. The slamming of the door echoed through the dumbstruck household. Maria's face was pale with anguish, what should she do?

Betsy was more practical, she organized a breakfast tray and told Lady Marchant's maid that her mistress had a headache and would not be seen this morning. Lady Marchant's maid was well acquainted with the morning's storm but she accepted the information as gravely as Betsy imparted it. Within an hour Lady Marchant knew all but the exact reason for the argument.

◆◆◆

Chapter 32

Light and darkness

The next two weeks were truly times of light and darkness for both Miranda and Benedict. Miranda walked to Willow house each day, spending many happy hours planning her establishment. Betsy had eagerly agreed to stay in Wiltshire with her mistress as she too was enjoying her plans for the future. Miranda was determined to enjoy her fine new life.

On occasion, the fury she felt at Benedict for daring to treat her that way rushed to the surface, at other times, she was sad for the loss of his love. It was hard for her to remember that this Benedict did not know her as she knew him, her love had grown over a longer time and she knew that he had risked his life for her, he did not. Then just as this train of thought softened her she would remember how he had belittled her saving of the Marchant family, his belief that the ship would have been discovered anyway, and although this was true she knew that it would have been many hundreds of years after White Hart Manor had been lost and the Marchant line had died out and her anger grew again.

For his part, Lord Benedict was filled with joy as more and more of the rich and fabulous cargo came to the surface, he thanked his luck that he had chosen to ship gold and precious stones rather than spices which would have been ruined in the wreck. Even while he was standing shoulder to shoulder with the salvage men, strong muscles straining as he heaved as heavy a load as the best of them, his mind was turning to his next voyages. The untamed part of his nature was as wild and adventurous as the youngest of the crew that had perished but his risks were on a level most could not understand and he reaped the rich rewards and knew it to be his rightful due.

When the night closed in his thoughts would turn unbidden to Miranda, her impudence! How dare she call him to account? At some level he knew her words to be true which is why they were so searingly painful. At another level he knew who she reminded him of, growing up with Lady Marchant meant that he never underestimated a woman. Lord Benedict was very careful to play his part as courtier even at such a time.

He knew well that the King could make or break a family overnight and he had written to his King immediately he knew the ship was found to beg leave to remain away from Court during the salvage operation. He had sent the King a generous gift of a golden bowl studded with emeralds, polished until it gleamed and wrapped in a velvet cloth of such dark forest green that it was almost black. It was the perfect backdrop for the bowl and even Henry who had been presented with such treasures all his life was moved to voice his pleasure at its beauty. Henry was gracious in his granting of the leave, he sent his good wishes and desire to see Lord Benedict at Court again soon. Henry was genuine in his sentiments, he often felt beleaguered by the never ending demands for favour and Lord Benedict did none of this.

As he commanded the loyal group who worked long hours without complaint, Lord Benedict assessed the treasures, looking for gifts of beauty for Lady Marchant and his sister. For Lady Marchant, he selected a heavy necklace of linked gold, the workmanship was exquisite and it needed a lady of stature to carry it off. For Maria, Lord Benedict chose a dainty dressing for her hair, it was not quite a circlet, not quite a tiara, but midway between the two; the generous sprinkling of diamonds sparkled in candlelight and the wrought silver was as delicate as lacework, Benedict rightly guessed that this would please his sister. Now he hesitated, was it appropriate to present a similar gift to Miranda? He felt a confusion, he did not wish to appear as if he was pressing to make her his mistress and she was not a relation. He mentally shook himself, to return home with gifts for all but the lady who had been the means of finding his ship? Indeed not. He remembered her happiness in finding herself the mistress of Willow House and settled his choice upon a pair of beautifully fashioned goblets, gold and circled with rubies at the base of the cup, a little smaller than usual, as if made for the delicate touch of a woman's hand. Without making any decisions, he also carefully stored away a perfectly oval ruby set in a fragile outline of gold, threaded upon a fine gold chain, it was a remarkable piece.

******

A visit from old friends of Lady Marchant gave her the opportunity to introduce Miranda as under her protection for the first time. The elderly Lord Hogan and his Lady were quite enchanted by Miranda's reading of the poem IF and they could not be satisfied until she had read it to them twice and Lord Hogan had read it himself. 'My Dear, you must not keep a talent like this to yourself, may I have the great pleasure of a copy of this poem to share with those who will be able to appreciate it?' As Lady Marchant was smiling her approval Miranda was happy to grant his request and stopped worrying about Rudyard Kipling for the last time, in this life she would be a revered poet and composer and protected friend of the Marchant Family. Mistress Glover of Willow House would be a lady of substance, learning and music. She felt pangs of longing when discussion turned quite naturally to Lord Benedict but no-one could ever have known from the serene expression on her face.

The descent into sleep was still difficult, at the point when reason would no longer hold back the tides of feeling, she knew that she would dream feverishly of Benedict's kiss and touch or she would wake in terror that the ship had sunk deeper taking him with it. Many miles away Lord Benedict dreamt that he walked in the gardens with a lady again but every time he tried to take her hand she faded away, leaving only the lingering scent of crushed lavender in his memory as he woke.

◆◆◆

Chapter 33
Coming home

Lord Benedict was so dark skinned after two weeks on the sea in the wind and sun that Maria teased him that a Spaniard had taken her brother's place. His black hose and jacket with embroidered silver edgings and a loose trim of snow white ermine certainly presented a breathtaking picture, very different to the wild figure that had made its way home on a weary horse. A welcome bath, lined with thick sheets to prevent splinters and filled with steaming water carried from the kitchen then strewn with the sweetest smelling herbs had done much to restore him.

His man had attended to him with the attention due to a homecoming hero and it was very much Lord Benedict the courtier who came down to eat with his adoring family and Miranda. She was so glad to see him that she felt only gratitude that he too seemed to want to forget the hard words that had passed between them at their last meeting and his bow and her returning curtsey were warm and cordial.

Lord Benedict ate with great pleasure and raised a glass of rich burgundy to his grandmother, 'A wonderful supper Grandmother, there is no table in the whole world I would prefer to dine at.' Lady Marchant bowed her thanks, even her stern expression was relaxed and happy. Lord Benedict told tales of the salvage, he was a gifted storyteller and they felt the excitement of the dangerous undertaking as well as the thrill as each treasure was brought to the surface. Lord Benedict said nothing of the thief who had been discovered with his pockets stuffed with gold coins, his end had been swift and Lord Benedict felt no pleasure in doing what he had needed to do. It had sobered the excited men, all knew they would be well rewarded for their work and that crossing Lord Benedict Marchant was not worth the risk.

It was not until Lord Benedict had heard Miranda and Maria play and sing and the best beeswax candles were lit in the late summer's evening that he revealed his gifts. 'Ladies, I know that we will never forget these momentous events but everyone here deserves a special keepsake.' As he spoke he bowed his head to each of the three ladies in turn and felt a rush of relief that he had included Miranda as was right and proper.

There was a general excitement, everyone watched Lady Marchant open the silk wrapped package first and there was awe and amazement at the boldness of the design, it suited her perfectly. Lady Marchant, for all her correctness, knew the same thrill as when she had received her first Court gown as a girl. She enjoyed a moment of thinking about appearing at Court in such a daring piece, even Ann Boleyn with her French hoods had seen nothing like this.

Maria treasured the luxurious feel of her deep red velvet package for a moment, 'My sister, our dear father would no doubt have given you your first jewels if he had been spared, I hope you will allow me the privilege.' Lady Marchant could not help but shed a single tear at his words but Maria was too excited and as the beautiful piece fell into her lap she was speechless. Miranda helped her arrange it on her pretty hair and a maid was sent running for a mirror. Maria turned her head to catch the candlelight and gasped as the diamonds sparkled, 'I shall treasure this all my life my brother' she said seriously but could not resist bursting out with, 'and it's the prettiest possible present, thank you!'

Now all eyes turned to Miranda, the heavy silk wrapping was carefully undone, as the golden goblets emerged the rubies gleamed richly in the candlelight. Miranda gently touched the rim and then lifted the goblet, admiring the weight and feel. 'For your new home Mistress Miranda, I hope I have chosen well?' Miranda smiled at him, 'nothing could have pleased me more Lord Benedict. I shall think of the giver with gratitude every time their beauty graces my table.' 'May I look at them?' Maria reached out for the other goblet and stroked the rubies, as it tilted towards her she exclaimed, 'there is something in here!' Benedict smiled as Maria passed the small embroidered pouch to Miranda. As she tipped the contents onto the tablecloth, it was as if a blaze of fire shone out from a puddle of molten gold, even Lady Marchant gasped, the beauty of the unique piece catching everyone by surprise. 'It is too much!' Miranda was so startled at his generosity and at owning such a stunning piece.

'Indeed Madam, it is not. The Marchants owe you so much and if I have ever forgotten that I would ask for your forgiveness.' In that moment, the last drop of resentment left Miranda and her heart was too full to speak, it mattered not though, words were not needed. In the morning, Miranda awoke with such happiness, she almost leapt from her bed and gathering up the goblets and her ruby necklace she took them back to bed and admired them in the beauty of the morning sunshine. Betsy was in fine form too, she bustled in with the fresh rosewater and a soft drying cloth. She had held the servants' hall enthralled with her description of the necklace early that morning and felt her currency rise accordingly. The servants had roundly scorned her hopes for her Lady and the Master of White Hart Manor but now they felt less certain, 'stranger things have happened' seemed a sensible position to take after a gift like that had been given. Servants often think they know all but of Miranda's part in the finding of the shipwreck they knew nothing.

'What shall I lay out for you Mistress?' It was one of Betsy's duties for sure but it also gave her a nice insight into the day's plans.

'I'll wear my dove grey gown Betsy, and for tonight please prepare my red silk with the gold embroidered bodice, it will look well as the setting for my necklace.'

'It will my Lady! Such a beautiful piece, I don't think that Anne Boleyn has such a ruby!… the Queen, I mean of course Mistress.' Betsy hurriedly covered up her unthinking words, it was not wise to show that your heart still held Queen Katherine sovereign. Miranda smiled, 'I know not how my ruby compares to others Betsy, I shall just enjoy its beauty.' Betsy had a feeling that Mistress Miranda didn't yet know that Lord Benedict wouldn't be there to see the gorgeous gown and the first wearing of the ruby necklace. Much as she was normally the first to pass on any interesting snippets, she decided not to be the one who took the glow of happiness from Miranda today, she would find out soon enough no doubt.

It was true that Lord Benedict's absence took some of the shine from the evening but Miranda, Lady Marchant and Lady Maria all arrived at table adorned in their most beautiful gowns to set off their gifts. Even though Benedict's place was empty he was still the most loved person at the table, Lady Marchant was far too wise a courtier herself to complain that the King had sent for her grandson. Benedict had certainly been too wise to mention that he had been at home for less than 16 hours when the summons had come. Instead he had sent his grateful thanks to the king and promised to set off within the hour, it had been too early to rouse the household.

◆◆◆

Chapter 34

Henry's Court

There could be no mistaking the genuine look of pleasure on the King's face, 'Benedict! You have been gone too long! Hunting has not been the same without you!'

Benedict ignored the tight smiles of the Howards and Seymours who had been the King's hunting companions that day and leapt up from where he had knelt to greet his King. 'Your Majesty! It is so good to be back, I feel quite wild to ride out after so long.'

'At dawn tomorrow Benedict I will ride beside you at a pace to make lesser men's hearts quail!' Jane Seymour's brother did not show even by the slightest facial expression that the King was already promised to ride out with Jane, the King's path must be made easy in all things.

'Indeed!' Benedict felt alive, he longed to race his finest horse at Henry's side, to run at the fences and ditches, taking chances that would indeed leave other men pale with fear. Long days of gentle manners with his family and the intense labour with the salvage team could all be forgotten in the wild chase, he often felt as a boy again in the King's company and knew this feeling to be reciprocated.

'Your Majesty, if you and my Lord Cromwell have any time while I am here, I would tell you of the White Hart. I have made maps of the whole coastline where she was wrecked to add to your work.' No gift could have pleased Henry more, mapping the coastline of his country to bring protection against its enemies was a passion of both Cromwell and the King, in an instant Henry's interest was caught. 'Send Cromwell to the map room' he commanded, and putting his arm around Lord Benedict's shoulder he walked away with him, leaving those who were to have spent the rest of the day in his company to exchange black looks or feel secretly relieved at being able to drop the courtier's mask for a few hours.

Even Henry, who was used to being centre of attention in all things, was caught up in Lord Benedict's excitement as he talked of the reefs and the tides that had brought the White Hart to grief. His maps were precise and as he talked he used them to bring the whole salvage operation to life. All three men knew well the language of charts and the sea and Cromwell too felt part of the camaraderie as he added a tale of a voyage that had battled with wild storms at that very point.

When they retired to Henry's own apartments to drink wine before dinner, Benedict was touched to see that the exquisite bowl he had sent Henry was on his writing table, to be enjoyed every day and not sent to the exchequer as a dry entry on a balance sheet. Henry enquired most kindly of Lady Marchant's health and that of Lady Maria. As they talked Henry was reminded of Lord Hogan who had been recently at Court.

'Indeed Benedict, I was most startled when Lord Hogan gave me a copy of the poem written by your grandmother's protégé, I know not when I have seen it's like, Sir Thomas Wyatt was quite out of sorts at first I can tell you. Now, like me, he has only curiosity about such talents, has she written other works?'

'She is a remarkable musician as well as poet My Lord, she sings and plays well but when she sings and plays songs she has composed herself it is like nothing I have heard before, quite captivating.' Benedict was lulled by the pleasure of

Henry's company and the wine, having known Henry all his life he should have known what was coming next, too late he realised.

'I am curious to meet such a lady, tell her we will be pleased to see her at Court' Henry was delighted with his own magnanimity. Benedict had spent the last few years keeping Maria safe from the snares of the Court and now he had thrown Miranda into its midst with one thoughtless sentence. He was too wise to try and change Henry's mind and was not trying to do so when he said, 'Mistress Glover will be much honoured My Lord, she may be a little out of her depth, she makes no secret of the fact that she is of humble birth although her father was a most learned scholar.'

'A scholar! Then indeed she is of higher birth than both my Archbishop and my Chancellor, the sons of the blacksmith and the butcher!' Henry roared with laughter and Benedict could not refrain from laughing too. Henry surely had his hands full with his increasingly bitter hatred of Anne Boleyn and his attentions towards Jane Seymour, knowing Henry he may have lost interest in Miranda even before she arrived. It was decided that Lady Marchant and Maria should accompany Miranda to Court and Lord Benedict dispatched a messenger to bid them make haste and advise his grandmother that Henry had ordered that the finest apartments should be put at her disposal.

◆◆◆

Chapter 35
The Royal Invitation

'Indeed Madam, I cannot!' Lady Marchant was rarely lost for words but she joined Maria in staring in astonishment at Miranda's outburst. 'I will not go, I will not!' Miranda ran from the room. After a moment's silence, Lady Marchant completely ignored the outburst and sent for her maid to instruct her to commence packing for herself and Lady Maria and to send word to Betsy to do the same for Mistress Glover.

The next morning the party set off at dawn in their travelling gowns although Lady Marchant very much intended that they should change into much finer gowns immediately they arrived at Court. The fine horses of the escort party set a brisk pace in the early cool of the day. Miranda was quiet but polite, her inner turmoil concealed by a calm face; Maria was beside herself with excitement, picturing herself being presented to the King and making her curtsey with such elegance and grace that the whole Court would take notice; Lady Marchant was still rather exasperated at the naivety of her protégé who had really seemed to believe that she was at liberty to say no to a royal invitation.

The beautiful gifts from the shipwreck were safely packed but Miranda had one extra piece with her, on a chain around her neck she carried the key to the secret door. Her one-time obsession with Henry had shriveled to nothing but fear that he would want her again in this dimension of time. She knew well that Benedict could not save her even if he was willing to risk the wrath of the King, what Henry wanted Henry got. The slow burn of love for Lord Benedict was now a deep and permanent fire in Miranda's very soul, she could not make herself available to Henry for the good of the Marchants, it would be a betrayal of Lord Benedict and all she felt for him. She would go back through the door before that happened and she would keep the means of doing that with her at all times. For a fleeting moment, she missed the girl who had fallen so hopelessly under Henry's spell, but she was gone now and could never come back.

The apartments reserved for Lady Marchant and her party were the very same that had been the scene of Miranda's joys when she had last stayed in the splendour of Greenwich Palace; the comfort of the familiar rooms bustling with energetic servants unpacking and preparing for the coming evening brought a smile to her face that even the apprehension she felt at meeting the King could not dampen. As soon as she was alone in her room she feverishly searched for her mother's pearls, in her rational mind she knew they could not be found but so many things had happened that defied reason that there was room for a tiny splinter of hope in her heart. It came to nothing but her spirits had lifted and she felt better able to deal with meeting Henry. All she needed to do was perform her poems and songs, stay modest and not meet fire with fire as she had last time. This would be no hardship as there was nothing but damp ash where that fire had once blazed, Miranda blushed to think of the passion she and Henry had shared and had to remind herself that it had never happened in this version of time. She was nothing to Henry, he was nothing to her.

The apartments were filled with steam, delicious scents of almond, lemon and honeysuckle, and frantic servants who rushed about shaking out beautiful gowns, mending embroidery on dancing slippers, filling and emptying wooden baths lined with heavy linen and laying out the beautiful jewels that would adorn the three ladies that night. Miranda caught up her music and poetry books and read them over and over, she started to feel as if the words and notes would fly straight out of her head when she was called upon to perform.

Betsy flitted in and out of the apartment as her old friends and relatives found pretexts to stop by, eventually Lady Marchant realised that Betsy was indeed a former maid of the Palace and raised an enquiring eyebrow at Miranda. 'Yes, I am fortunate in my maid.' Miranda was telling no lies and did not offer to expand further. Lady Marchant knew that there was a mystery here and threw Miranda a sharp look. Time was pressing though and the subject was left alone.

When Lord Benedict arrived to escort the party to the gathering in the Great Hall, the ladies were arrayed in such finery that even he caught his breath at his first sight of them. His Marchant heart swelled with pride as he saw his grandmother who carried herself with an elegance of bearing that brought Queen Katherine herself to mind; her necklace with the crafted gold links was startling in its absolute difference to anything ever seen at Court before. Maria was breathtaking in her innocence and beauty, a powder blue gown edged with silver thread at bodice and sleeves was set off exquisitely by the silver and diamond head dress; as she moved the light caught every diamond and it was as if tiny stars hovered above her. It was when he allowed himself to really look at Miranda that Benedict knew that he loved her. The ruby necklace lay at her throat, its purity of colour and light the perfect adornment to the deepest red silk gown that showed off her grace and soft curves to perfection. Her caramel blonde hair was softly braided and looped under her crescent hood, trimmed with the prettiest of seed pearls.

As their party entered the Great Hall, Miranda's touched the fine chain around her neck, reassuring herself that the key was still there, hidden beneath the bodice of her gown. The ruby necklace drew every eye and the fine gold chain was invisible in contrast to it. Looking towards the secret alcove, Miranda felt a painful pull towards it, her old life and Alice were so very close, in literally minutes she could walk towards the tube and be travelling across London. This life held so much potential for danger, how on earth had she ended up in a situation where she was in real danger of incurring the wrath of the King again? Then Benedict smiled at her, seemingly oblivious to the interested looks from many of the ladies of the Court, with eyes only for her. No, it was time to make a choice and make a stand, if there was any way she could be with Benedict without bringing down the Marchant family or risking her own life then she was staying. The key was the last resort.

Behind his courtier's smile, Benedict wished with all his being that Miranda's beauty could be only in the eye of the beholder and that Henry would not see her as he saw her. It was not to be, two hours later, as lord Benedict watched Henry bow to Miranda and raise her from her seat at the virginal where she had played her music that had touched the very spirit of the whole Court, he knew that life was taking a different turn. Above all Henry loved music and when a kindred spirit presented itself in the form of a beautiful young woman he was his best self. Even so he was King and it rarely occurred to him that what he desired would not be his. He offered Miranda his arm and asked her to walk in the gardens with him, where the scents of late summer were heady and pools of red and gold lamplight lit up the shadows.

◆◆◆

Chapter 36
The King's intentions

In the morning melee comprised of the courtiers, grooms, horses and hunting dogs, there was a still moment lasting some seconds where Sir William Carey caught Benedict's eye and his gaze was a curious mixture of empathy and contempt. Lord Benedict felt disturbed, Sir William had been the recipient of many such glances and murmurs when the King had taken a liking to his young wife Mary Boleyn. The Careys had been married but a short time and all men bar the King knew what it had cost for Sir William to stand by and bow and smile as the King had taken his new young wife for his mistress. Henry saw no reason why he should not hunt and joust with his great favourite Sir William after rising from the bed of his pretty young wife Mary. Mary had been put aside when her sister Anne rose in favour of course but for William the happiness of his marriage was forever tainted, no matter how many rich rewards his King had granted him. As his groom helped him mount his glorious chestnut stallion, Henry shouted, 'Benedict! ride with me!' As they rode away with the others of the party streaming out behind them the King was exuberant, 'So Benedict, you hide such a treasure from me! Tell me have you known Mistress Glover long?' There was no mistake, William Carey knew it and no doubt so did all the other courtiers, the King wanted Miranda.

The courtier's mask never slipped for a second. 'Indeed Your Majesty, I have met her on but a few occasions. My grandmother formed the acquaintance some months since and agreed to be Mistress Glover's friend and guardian, she did discuss it with me but it was pretty much all arranged.

You have known my grandmother this many years My Lord.' This last was said with the wry expression of a man who knows that he has met his match.

Henry laughed, 'I have indeed known your grandmother these many years, I would take her counsel in all things, if she has decided to take Mistress Glover into the fold of the Marchants then the lady must be a rare treasure to warrant such an honour.' Henry watched Benedict keenly, 'And do you think that Mistress Glover might like to spend a little longer at Court? She seems modest and would not I think ask for preference for herself.'

There was nothing else for it, 'Your Majesty, I have no doubt that she would be most honoured to know she was welcomed, my Lady Grandmother will manage all plans for a longer stay with much pleasure I am sure.' Benedict's smile was open, Henry could never have guessed the turmoil that lay beneath his words. 'She is modest and maidenly in her manner Your Majesty, she has led a life of scholarship and her mind is much caught up in music and poetry.' Benedict was doing all he could to buy Miranda some time, Henry's own view of himself as a chivalrous prince meant that he would never bring pressure to bear on a maiden. At the very least this may mean that Henry courted Miranda instead of sending for her that very night. The hunting horn sounded and Henry and Benedict broke into a gallop, all desires and worries forgotten for a few hours at least. It was late afternoon before Benedict arrived at Lady Marchant's magnificent apartments with the invitation to join the King's party at the joust the following day. Lady Marchant was much pleased with the honour done to her family, less than twenty four hours was barely enough to ensure that their finery reflected their position but done it must be and seamstresses and milliners were sent for that very moment.

Betsy could hardly believe her luck, she had left the Palace as a general lady's maid, allocated to any Lady who was without her own and now she was in the thick of it. All knew that the King's attention had turned to Miranda and Betsy was already preparing a sleeping mask of herbs and oils that would see her wake with the softest skin and fairest complexion.

'Walk with me Mistress Miranda,' Lord Benedict spoke quietly, only Miranda heard him and with a brief curtsey to Lady Marchant she joined him in a walk in the palace gardens alongside the river. He found it hard to speak, 'Mistress Miranda…'

'I know, he wants me' Miranda's face betrayed no emotion, but her voice said all that Benedict needed to know. This was no girl out to win the King's heart for her own advancement or for foolish dreams of love, Miranda wanted none of it. 'I will not submit to him, I will disappear from Court and from all things before he lays hand on me Lord Benedict. I will go and none shall see me again,'

'Miranda,' Lord Benedict hesitated, 'The King's favour is no small thing to be turned aside lightly, his anger is no small thing to incur either.'

Miranda stopped walking and turned towards him, there was no-one within hearing distance, the group playing quoits was some little distance away. 'Do you want me to gain the King's favour in this manner Benedict? Please tell me plain.'

Lord Benedict, felt a spasm of feeling tear through him, it was so sharp it was almost grief, he did not answer, he laid her delicate hand on his arm and walked determinedly towards the high hedges of the pretty shrubbery, as soon as they were out of sight of all he grasped her hand and swung her around to face him, fiercely he pulled her towards him, holding her close and tight. He breathed in the heady scent of her perfume and kissed the hollow at the side of her neck so softly that her skin shivered in response and anticipation, his lips moved up her neck, his hands entwined in her hair, he held her softly but as if he'd never let her go. As his lips found hers their lips parted and the intensity of their kiss was matched by the involuntary murmurs that escaped them both, the full length of their bodies coming together so Miranda could feel his heart beating desperately. 'I cannot bear it, I cannot bear for anyone else to have you Miranda, not the King not anyone.' His voice was hoarse, 'do you feel the same?' He kissed her again, deep and hungry, caught in longing even though they were but yards from sight and could be disturbed at any moment. 'I want only you My Lord, I know not how I can escape the King but he will not have me, I promise you.' Lord Benedict lowered his lips to the neckline of her light silk gown, pulling at the soft fabric with his mouth, her murmurings encouraged him even though he knew it was madness. 'Benedict, Benedict, more' she moaned as she felt quite desperate to have him right there in the shrubbery with the lords and ladies of the Court strolling on the other side of the hedge. Shockingly, he suddenly pulled up her dress, as she panted and groaned he whispered in her ear, 'Dare I risk it here and now Miranda?' His eyes never left hers as he whispered to her, wild and dangerous words that were more often spoken by candlelight. The sounds of the Quoits players arguing a point reached them on the warm air. He could no longer bear it, he pulled her into the thickest part of the shrubbery and together they fell onto the long grass 'I can't wait Miranda, I'm sorry' he gasped. She lost all sense of time and place and at one point she realised that he had covered her mouth with his hand to stop her crying out. At last, they lay in exhausted silence for a few moments, listening to the conversation of two ladies in waiting as they passed so close that a moment's turn of direction would have brought them face to face with an unexpected afternoon tableau.

As they hurriedly brushed off grass and adjusted their clothing Benedict picked a perfect creamy bloom from a camellia bush, 'This is our marriage Miranda, you are mine now. None shall have you, I will set my mind to find a way out of our dilemma.' 'My Lord, we must have lost our minds, let us return quickly before Lady Marchant sends a search party.' 'But you are mine?' His voice was urgent and serious. 'For all time, across the centuries.' Miranda too was serious, they kissed a gentle kiss and stepped out around the shrubbery back towards the Palace. 'Just one request My Lord' Miranda looked up at his handsome face as they strolled across the chamomile lawn with perfect decorum. 'Anything, name it'

'At some point, do you think we could conduct some of our courtship indoors?'

◆◆◆

Chapter 37

The call of destiny

Lady Marchant had dismissed all the servants and sent Maria to bed to ensure that she had complete privacy for her talk with Miranda. 'My Dear, you have been greatly honoured by the King's attentions, I believe that he may request a private meeting with you if all goes well at the joust tomorrow. It will be a fine thing for you if he does.'

As she poured two goblets of rich red wine with her own hands, Lady Marchant was not as calm as she appeared, the Court was a dangerous place and Anne Boleyn had no love for a woman who had been such a staunch friend to Queen Katherine. Henry's tastes had obviously turned to the sweeter looks and gentler natures of girls such as Jane Seymour and Miranda; the hard, glittering allure of Anne Boleyn had worn very thin of late.

The Seymours were not threatened by the King's obvious interest in a nobody, it was a temporary irritant, nothing more. Even so, it hardly endeared them to Lady Marchant and she faced frosty bows and bland faced curtseys in many quarters. Lady Marchant returned all such slights with the dignity fitting to her position and ancestry but she noted every change of alliance and stored away the information to use in the service of the king or the Marchants.

'How so will it be a fine thing Lady Marchant? I do not seek private audience with the King, I do not want his attentions.' Miranda tried hard to be as calm as Lady Marchant but her voice betrayed fear or anger, possibly both. Her hand clenched white around her goblet.

'Miranda, your future will be secured if you have the King's favour, your small fortune now will be as nothing to the manors and lands that may be granted to you. His interest will soon wane, you will not be troubled for long. If he should get you with child your line will benefit for generations to come.' Lady Marchant was long schooled in pragmatism and action that may not reap rewards until many years hence, the Marchants thought in terms of generations. She was a little exasperated that Miranda seemed unable to realise what an opportunity had presented itself to her.

'And what if I should wish to marry Lady Marchant? Will any husband accept such a situation?'

'Certainly, if he has any sense and you certainly don't want a husband without any.' Lady Marchant had very definite views on husbands.

'Lady Marchant...It is not for me to say, Lord Benedict will speak to you.'

There was silence, 'do not be foolish Miranda, if you have feelings for Benedict then do not ruin his life, he can marry the highest in the land now and above all he must serve his King, if that includes losing to him in the bedchamber then so be it.' Her voice was not without sympathy, she too had been young once and her past held secrets that would never be divulged.

'I beg you to talk with Lord Benedict Lady Marchant, I cannot find the words to describe the love I feel for him, it comes but once in a lifetime. I would do nothing to hurt him ever, but I would betray my very soul if I was to turn from him now.'

There was silence, 'I will speak with my grandson, you may retire.' Miranda swept Lady Marchant a deep curtsey. As

Miranda closed her bedroom door, her tears flowed silently, as she sobbed Betsy helped her undress and gently bathed her face in the warm rosewater. By the time Betsy was soothingly brushing her hair, the storm had passed and only the odd tear still escaped. Betsy was too wise a lady's maid to pass comment, she helped her Lady into her nightshift and sprinkled the pillow and sheets with lavender water before quietly leaving the room.

Lord Benedict was jolted with shock when Lady Marchant entered his apartments, for her to arrive so late and unannounced signaled great urgency. 'Grandmother! What is it? Is Maria ill? Miranda?' He grasped her hands and helped her to a high backed chair, upholstered with a rich tapestry of the White Hart on a burgundy background, nodding to his servant to pour her some reviving wine. Lady Marchant took the wine and imperceptibly motioned to Benedict to dismiss the servant. This was done with all haste and Lord Benedict drew up a stool close to his grandmother, 'tell me.'

'Miranda, explain'

Lord Benedict flushed red, it was one thing to swear undying love for Miranda and swear to protect her against all comers in the glow of love, another to explain it to his grandmother who put duty to the family and King above all things. Lady Marchant listened in impassive silence while Lord Benedict spoke of his love for Miranda, how he had felt nothing like this before and knew it would not come again, of his need to protect her but at the same time how he drew strength from her very presence, how he wanted her to be the mother of his children.

Eventually there was silence, then 'Benedict, there is nothing you have said that cannot be achieved by making Miranda your mistress, she must understand that the best match possible for you can now be achieved'.

'Grandmother, let me ask you a question, what if best did not mean wealthiest or most powerful? What is best meant that you had heard a call of destiny, one that could not be ignored without losing something of your very self?' Benedict's voice was impassioned and low, he could not sit, he paced the chamber, as if it was too small to hold all his feelings and his inability to express them in a way that Lady Marchant could understand.

'A call of destiny? Is this really how it is for you Benedict?' Lady Marchant stared intently at him, 'speak truly now.'

'With all my heart Madam, this is truly how it is, help me Grandmother, I know not what to do.' Benedict collapsed into the chair opposite Lady Marchant.

There was a long silence, then Lady Marchant said, 'I must think, the King is our immediate problem, you must let me think for the Marchants Benedict, your blood is too hot to think clearly, give me your word you will do nothing rash.'

Benedict felt the relief flow through his body, he knelt before his grandmother's chair and kissed her hand with deep gratitude, 'you have my word Grandmother, you have my word.'

Many hours later, when Lady Marchant had endured an even later visit from the Queen's sister, Lady Mary Carey who would always be Boleyn through and through, she mused on how much easier it would be if she could just tell Mary that they were all united in their desire to keep Henry away from Miranda. It never paid to enter into any sort of alliance or confidence with a Boleyn though and Lady Marchant kept her counsel. Mary reported back that the nobody had been nowhere to be seen which sent the Queen into a frenzy of suspicion and fury and could not be calmed until the small hours.

◆◆◆

Chapter 38
Friend and Protector

'Miranda, I expect you to follow my advice without question, do we understand each other?' Lady Marchant's first words to Miranda on the day of the joust took her by surprise, at first the instinct to obey a voice of such authority over-rode all else so it was a moment or two before she responded.

'Indeed Lady Marchant, I will follow no advice from you or anyone else without question. Pray tell me where you expect your advice to lead and I will decide if I will follow it.'

At that moment, Lady Marchant's maid entered the room, the tension was such that she turned around and left again without even dropping a curtsey.

'You foolish girl, you expect my help and yet will not listen to me!'

'Lady Marchant, are you saying that you will help us?' Miranda's voice unstiffened enough to show a tiny sliver of hope.

Lady Marchant suddenly relaxed, 'sit down my dear, I have been turning ideas over in my mind all night, I forget that you do not know that Benedict and I have talked. I will help you, but you must trust me, I cannot be second guessed on all things, and I will not explain all.'

Miranda relaxed too, she walked over to the window where Lady Marchant stood framed against the morning sunshine, impulsively she took her hand and held it to her cheek, 'Thank you, thank you.' There was a moment's silence, the dust motes danced in the light of the day, the scents of sweet peas and honeysuckle drifted in, eventually Lady Marchant cleared her throat,

'Well, standing here will move us no further on. Maria, Elspeth, Betsy!'

The next few hours passed in a flurry of activity as Lady Marchant marshalled her forces, gowns were shaken out and trimmed; basins were filled with the freshest and lightest of scented waters; rose and lilac fragrances filled the rooms as they were sprinkled on gleaming hair and pretty necks and shoulders. Both Maria and Miranda wore ribbons and seed pearls at their necks and their crescent hoods were braided ribbons of silk in the Marchant colours of burgundy and Ivory. They were absolutely delicious, Maria in palest lavender trimmed with Ivory silk at the bosom and sleeves and Miranda in shot silk ivory with slim insets of burgundy in the full skirt and burgundy ruffles at the shoulders.

Maria was allowed to listen in as Lady Marchant drilled Miranda on how she should deal with the King at the joust, at all times she was to be shy but adoring. At no time was she to be alone with him, on no account was she to be flirtatious, while still showing admiration and devotion. Any opportunities to speak of her own father were to be taken. Miranda wouldn't have been human if she hadn't felt a huge thrill of pleasure from how beautiful she looked. As she moved she felt her gown rustle softly as it flowed from the fitted bodice. She felt so elegant, the world of her own time was passing from her, her passing thoughts of her old life were almost dreamlike. Lady Marchant crossed the room and opened her own private silver box with a small key she wore around her neck, Miranda touched her own key which hung beneath her dress on a chain so fine it could not be seen. Did all ladies have their secrets? Lady Marchant removed a tiny phial of glass and silver from a velvet inlaid compartment, it brought the oil that had driven Henry so wild in a different dimension of time sharply to mind. 'I'm not sure how this is going to lessen the King's interest Lady Marchant?'

'You just leave that to me Miranda, your role is to adore, respect and admire but never, ever flirt, not even a glance from beneath your lashes, are we in agreement?'

'No Lady Marchant, I must know what is being done, I am marrying into your family and I must be trusted.'

'It is not a matter of trust Miranda, the family recipes are known only to my female line, we do not ride to battle but we protect our line and make our gains as well as any Lord who ever graced a battlefield. Maria has been schooled in the making of our recipes and it is her inheritance, those not of our blood must not be allowed to dilute our power by sharing our secrets with their own families.' Lady Marchant was not over stern, the resolute and courageous Miranda awoke an echo of her own younger days.

'I am twice a Marchant now Madam, once by virtue of my betrothal to Benedict and again by your agreement to protect me. I am not of your blood but I have no other kin and no division of loyalties. I am sworn to the Marchants throughout time.' There was a depth of truth in Miranda's tone that stilled the room,

Lady Marchant hesitated and then swiftly made her decision. 'I will tell you what this will do but I will give you no recipe for it, I will not give any part of Lady Maria's inheritance away without her full consent.' 'And other recipes, Your Ladyship?' Miranda knew that the oils to keep Benedict forever at her side were in that box, his mother may have had to suffer the impertinence of a Mistress in the grounds of her Manor but she felt very certain that Lady Marchant herself had suffered no such insult. 'Enough Madam, do not over reach yourself, and do not assume that Maria will agree or indeed that I will advise her to, it is an inheritance of no small value.'

Miranda curtseyed her apologies and Lady Marchant nodded her acceptance and opened the phial, carefully she dabbed the colourless and seemingly odourless liquid behind Miranda's ears, at the nape of her neck and on her wrists, then she sprinkled a minuscule amount over her hair, 'have you seen the love of a mother for her newborn Miranda? A pure and protective love that makes all other loves seem as the lightest breeze when compared to the hurricane of the storm? When a new child is born to a woman of my line the baby is anointed with this recipe before the household and knights swear allegiance. As they kneel to the new child of the house they are overwhelmed with the love and protective instinct that is given to a new mother, but magnified and multiplied many times. The recipe will hold its power but two hours but the instincts once awakened will hold for all time. Those knights and yeomen must be ready to gladly die in the service of the House as they may well be called upon to do so. Anyone who comes close to you today will feel the love and protective instinct of a father or a brother, this is my gift to you and to Benedict.'

Miranda looked at Lady Marchant in astonishment, to think that her great, great grandmothers had been experimenting with pheromones centuries ago and with such incredible results. Miranda had no doubt it would work, memories of the first night she had spent with Henry still had the power to send tremors through her body in an unguarded moment. 'But be warned Miranda, if you want Benedict to love you as a man loves a woman then you must stay well away from him today, otherwise he will see you as a sister and will be filled with horror if you see him as aught but a brother.' Miranda curtseyed her understanding, she rose just as Lord Benedict entered the room and he felt as if he was seeing her again for the first time, an absolute vision that made even his courtier's greeting die on his lips.

Fortunately, Maria whirled into the room just at that moment 'what do you think brother? This time last week I was walking in the orchard at home with only the sheep and goats to see me! Today I will sit in the King's pavilion wearing the prettiest gown in London!'

Even Lady Marchant could not keep up her strict demeanour in the face of such happiness and Benedict laughed aloud, 'I am the most fortunate man in all the Court, my party consists of the three most beautiful ladies wearing the three most elegant gowns ever seen at a joust, I shall be the envy of all and they will heartily long for me to be knocked from my horse!'

Lord Benedict was most certainly adding to the overall splendour of his party himself, he wore the dashing burgundy and ivory tunic that marked his jousting appearances, with his broad shoulders and muscled arms he looked well today, he was dressed ready for his groom to help him into his armour. He gave his arm to Lady Marchant and she felt a swell of pride as she saw many eyes turn to her family as they crossed the immaculate lawns towards the gaily striped red and white pavilions, there was many a titled Mama taking a great interest in Lord Benedict and he had been long enough at Court to know that they weren't all thinking about husbands for their daughters. The gentlemen of Court were chivalrous in their homage to beauty as Miranda and Maria followed on and there were many bows and smiles. Fortunately Maria was very happy to dawdle a little and did not try to rush Miranda to catch up with her brother and grandmother when she seemed to slow her pace. Maria could not help but blush as she saw the handsome young squire who had caught her eye earlier in the week, circle around the edge of the throng to place himself in perfect position to bow to her, she dropped a dainty curtsey and was rewarded by seeing him blush too, although nothing could hide the irrepressible mischief that danced in his every glance.

As they approached the pavilion, the chatter of conversation suddenly changed to a focused murmur, all eyes turned towards the Marchants now. No-one could mistake the look of genuine joy on the King's face as he left the pavilion to greet his guests, he raised Lady Marchant from her faultless curtsey and gave her his arm, his smile and welcome encompassing the whole party. When the ladies were all seated in a cool and comfortable spot and Lord Benedict had excused himself to get ready for the jousting, the King quietly asked Miranda if she would like to see his horse.

She looked at him with open adoration, 'Your Majesty! Thank you, we would love to although Lady Marchant may prefer the cool of the pavilion', as she rose, Maria rose with her, shining with happiness, it was impossible for Henry to exclude Maria from the invitation without being unchivalrous and when Henry's temper was sunny, no-one could resist his warmth. With great courtesy, the King offered each lady an arm and found himself thoroughly enjoying their company as he extolled the virtues of his gleaming chestnut stallion. He was delighted by the genuine admiration from the ladies and he laughed heartily at Maria's knowledge of his jousting success, 'I see you have marked my progress Lady Maria! Now tell me, am I your favourite to win today?' For a second Miranda worried that Maria should have had some of the clear liquid too but all of

Henry's best qualities were to the fore today. As Maria hesitated Henry said with delight, 'I do hope that it is the thought of your brother that makes you hesitate Lady Maria?', 'Indeed it is Your Majesty, but I think that I must be allowed to place my brother just a little behind my King or would that be unsisterly?' Nothing could have pleased Henry more, he roared with laughter and assured Maria that he would make such a thing right with her brother.

As they returned to the pavilion he thought to ask Miranda how she liked being part of the Marchant family, 'When my father died your Majesty, I felt such sorrow at having no protector, no-one who would care for me as my dear father had. To have such as Lady Marchant to be my friend and to guide me in the world has been a blessing I could not have foreseen, I give thanks for her every day in my prayers.'

Henry was quite taken aback to find himself so moved, he felt emotion surge through him, 'On my honour Mistress Miranda, will you count me as friend and protector too? To think of you out in the world alone would grieve me sorely, the Marchants have been as close as blood to me and Lady Marchant has been my safe harbour when I have been tired and weary, I would stand friend for her kin always'. Henry had stopped walking and looked seriously at Miranda as he spoke, she looked up at him and as her tears of gratitude fell she knew that it was done and that she could never repay Lady Marchant as long as she lived.

◆◆◆

Chapter 39

Inheritance

The sun had barely risen the next morning when Lord Benedict arrived at his grandmother's apartments, 'Well Grandmother, do you intend to tell me how you did it?' Lady Marchant allowed herself a small smile, 'what has happened?'

'The King began by ordering me to find Miranda a husband but within minutes he had decided that nothing could please him but that she should be my own bride! He mistook my astonishment for reluctance and gave me a lecture on how I should indeed be married at my age and if I couldn't see that my grandmother had found me a wife worthy of a Marchant I hadn't half her wit or wisdom!'

Even Lady Marchant could not help but laugh, 'I assume you acknowledged the superiority of your dear Grandmother?' Benedict was suddenly serious, 'Always, never a day goes by when I don't give thanks for all you do for me and our dear Maria. I will not ask you how you have made this happen but I do know that my happiness is owed to you.' He knelt at Lady Marchant's feet and she quietly gave him her blessing. 'Now Benedict, I think that the lavender walk is the prettiest place in the gardens, it may be that Miranda would appreciate some delightful morning air.'

It would have been a delightful place for a marriage proposal, with the delicious scents of lavender forever destined to bring back the moment when Benedict told Miranda that the King approved, no indeed, positively insisted, that they should marry. Instead, Benedict pulled Miranda into a shadowy alcove immediately outside the door of Lady Marchant's apartments where he scattered tiny kisses on Miranda's eyelids, ears and forehead and in between kisses she heard the news that would bind them together for all time. They did eventually walk to the lavender walk, Miranda's arm through Benedict's and their happiness so evident that the early risers smiled at the lovers.

Anne Boleyn and Mary watched them curiously from a high window, eventually the Queen said, 'I would wager we are mistaken this time Mary.' And Mary nodded her agreement.

******

The eve of the wedding saw a curious scene at White Hart Manor. Miranda, Maria and Lady Marchant dismissed the servants and checked that all the windows were closed and that no-one stood behind the hangings. Then they gathered at the oak dining table and lit the candles. In the golden pool of light with all darkness beyond it, Maria opened the proceedings. 'Miranda, I shall stand as sister to you for as long as I shall live, tomorrow I will give you the precious oil that will bind my brother to you, and you to him, for all time in the marriage bed, this is a solemn thing that I do, never before has a woman not of my grandmother's maternal line been allowed to use the secret recipe.'

Miranda was quite awed by this different Maria, the sweet girl was gone, the steeliness of the Marchants showed through, she was in deadly earnest. 'However, I shall not teach you our recipes, that is my inheritance to be given to my own daughters when I am blessed, I shall not lessen their power, I do not have the right and I do not have the inclination.'

Miranda raised her goblet to her lips, her mind was racing, the thought of what was to come tomorrow night after she had slowly rubbed the oil into Benedict's muscular shoulders made her shiver in anticipation, but this was no time to get lost in such thoughts. 'And what of my daughters when I am blessed?' Miranda had no need to say that the blood of Lady Marchant's ancestors would flow through her line too.

Maria softened, 'that is my wedding gift to you Miranda, if my grandmother should die before she can teach your daughters what they need to know I undertake to pass on the hidden knowledge, I will not stint, your daughters will have the same ancient knowledge I will give my own when we are blessed.'

A deep look passed between Lady Marchant and Lady Maria, even now, the name of Lilith, the first of their line, could not be spoken before one not of their blood.

Unusually, Lady Marchant had been silent throughout the whole conversation, now she asked a question, 'I see you have asked Benedict to buy you 180 hectares of land to the west of London as a wedding gift, what has possessed you to desire such rough fields my dear? The farmland around your own Willow House will yield richer crops.'

Miranda smiled, 'if there is one thing I have learned from you Lady Marchant it is to think of my line for many years to come, I believe that this land could in time be used for the May Fair celebrations. It will be left entailed to the bloodline in perpetuity so none shall ever be without a place to call home; who knows what the May Fair land shall become in time?' And knowing that tomorrow night would be spent with Benedict at Willow House, with the glow of candles softly lighting their room as her wedding dress slipped from her shoulders and her husband was bound to her for all time in a fever of desire, she went to bed as Mistress Glover for the very last time.

The end

If you would like to be the first to know when the next Marchant Dynasty novel is published please email spearmint@manx.net and ask to be added to the 'First to know' list.

Printed in Great Britain
by Amazon